Cadaver Lab

A ROMANTIC COMEDY... WITH CORPSES

CAT JOHNSON

Chapter One

"THIS IS LUCY SUNSHINE FROM WBNG NEWS. Binghamton New York's finger on the pulse of the Southern Tier. I'm coming to you today from Mudville where one local shop owner has a *shocking* tale to tell.

"Here with me now is Natalie Chase, owner of Once Upon a Vine, the book and wine shop behind us. But the store is not Ms. Chase's claim to fame. That stems from a recent event that will really *spark* your interest. Ms. Chase, can you tell us about it?"

Thrusting the microphone in front of Natalie's mouth, the pretty dark-haired woman waited expectantly.

The reporter's smile remained large, frozen in time, as the seconds of silence ticked by.

Lucy Sunshine finally shifted her gaze from the

camera lens to Natalie, also frozen where she stood shoulder-to-shoulder with the reporter.

"Ms. Chase?"

Next to her, Once Upon a Vine's part-time employee Jules—short for Julia—stomped hard on Natalie's foot while smiling for the camera.

That was enough to yank Natalie's attention away from the large—as in *large*—crowd of people circling her as her mind turned to the pain in her foot.

But still she couldn't help wondering. Were there even this many people living in this town? Was Lucy Sunshine so famous her fans had flocked here to see her?

Maybe WBNG had bussed them in for the shot.

"Can you tell us what happened to you on that *electrifying* night last week?" the reporter repeated her question with her ever-present smile in place and her eyes on the camera lens.

"Uh..." That was all Natalie managed.

She probably looked like a deer in headlights as she too stared at the camera while trying to ignore the hoards that seemed to be closing in on her.

The crowd pressed closer, but Lucy Sunshine's smile didn't waver as she continued, "Two nights ago, during the storm predicted so accurately by our own precision weather forecaster Stormy Jones, you exited your shop and then what happened?"

The reporter had stopped talking again.

Panicked, Natalie shot her a sideways glance. Had there been a question in there? Oh, right. What happened. What *had* happened?

"Um…"

"Didn't you, while you were outside of your shop in an attempt to rescue your cat and dog from the storm, sustain a severe electrocution when a downed power line hit the puddle you'd stepped in?"

"*Not* my cat. Or my dog," she managed, realizing she was sounding like a crazy cat lady on TV.

Ignoring the mumbled comment, Lucy Sunshine forged ahead undaunted. "And according to the first-hand account of your employee, you were technically dead for approximately three and a half minutes. In fact, she reported to rescue workers upon their arrival that it was only the efforts of Doctor William Walsh, who'd seen the incident occur and performed CPR to restart your heart, that enabled you to be standing here with us today."

"Hmph. I guess," Natalie grunted begrudgingly since Doctor William Walsh had proven to be a self-centered a-hole.

But she couldn't worry about him now as one of the onlookers, an elderly woman in an outfit that had to be vintage, reached out and touched her sleeve.

Natalie pulled her arms closer, closing in on herself protectively. Meanwhile, some of the onlookers had started to mumble among themselves.

The din surrounding her grew louder.

Why wasn't the crew asking them all to stand back and be quiet? And why were these people so interested in her anyway?

"Dr. Walsh was unavailable for comment. Probably out there saving more lives," Lucy Sunshine said directly to the camera. "So there you have it, folks. A tragedy averted thanks to one good Samaritan. Remember to watch WBNG for the most accurate storm reports and avoid those puddles. This is Lucy Sunshine. Have a sunshiny day."

"And come to Once Upon a Vine for ten percent off a bottle of wine with any book purchase," Jules shouted that rapid fire promo offer toward the camera while leaning in front of Natalie.

"And we're out," one crew member said.

The on-air smile gone, Lucy Sunshine of WBNG shot Natalie a distinctly judgmental glare before strutting toward the news van.

That censure was probably meant to shame Natalie for being such a bad interviewee, but she couldn't worry about that. The press of people around her had become unbearable.

Meanwhile, Jules was speaking to her. Something about how the reporter could have talked about the shop more, but at least she'd be able to post the interview on their social media.

Natalie was only partially listening as the crowd parted and an attractive, middle-aged man possibly in his late forties, maybe early fifties, stepped directly in front of her. He was so close that his nose was barely a few inches away from hers as he stared directly into her face.

He was dressed in brown cargo pants and over a blue shirt with its sleeves rolled to the elbows he wore a vest that had at least as many pockets as his pants.

Completing the outfit were hiking boots and an Indiana Jones-style hat from beneath which intense blue eyes peered at her.

With forty breathing down her neck while she was woefully single, she wasn't opposed to dating an older man, especially an attractive one, but this aggressiveness on his part was too much.

Even if the most male-female action she'd gotten in far too long was the annoying but hot doctor giving her CPR while she'd been dead, she didn't go for pushy men. This guy was being just that.

Tired of wondering what was going on and even more tired of having her personal space invaded, she took a single step back as she said, "Can I help you?"

His eyes widened. "Oh my God. She can see us!" He'd directed the last part of his statement to the crowd behind him.

A cheer went up through those assembled.

Meanwhile, Jules replied to Natalie's question meant for the stranger, "Thanks. I don't need help. I'll just go see if they can email the link for the interview to me, then I'll post it."

"*I* need your help," the man said, stepping closer again as Jules headed in the opposite direction, leaving Natalie alone in this disturbing encounter.

"Who are you?" she asked.

"I'm Gabe. But that doesn't matter. What matters is that I was murdered and you're the only person who can help me find who did it."

Her mouth opened in realization. "Oh. Is this some sort of murder mystery book club? You're going to have to get on the calendar if you want to meet here."

If they all attended the meeting, she'd have to arrange for more chairs. The other book clubs only had a handful of attendees. She had to wonder how this club attracted so many members.

And they were really dedicated too. Now that she looked closer, quite a few of them appeared to be in costume, dressed in clothing from different eras.

A few even sported fake injuries. An axe in the head. A bloody slit throat. A gunshot wound to the chest.

She needed to expand the murder mystery section and advertise to these people. She'd known mystery and thriller was a big market but apparently the genre had truly enthusiastic fans.

"This is not a book club. I was murdered!" Gabe said with feeling.

"Okay, okay. Fine. I'll play along, but the meeting room is booked for today—"

"Look at me!" he shouted then spun around to reveal a literal knife in his back.

"Good prop. We're going to have to plan something with you guys at the shop for Halloween. Maybe a murder mystery party. Jules, do you see this?"

"Sorry, Nat. Are you talking to me?" At Jules's confused question, Natalie glanced over and saw her employee was still off to the side talking to one of the crew.

"Never mind. We'll talk later." She turned back to the guy. "Do you have a card or something?"

"Lady, I don't know what you don't understand. I'm dead. We're all dead." He circled one finger to indicate the rest of the crowd.

She rolled her eyes. "Yeah, yeah. You're dead. Look I respect your method acting or whatever but—"

With a frustrated groan the man walked directly at her. And then *through* her, leaving in his wake a tingling that she had to admit wasn't entirely unpleasant.

Frowning, she spun around to face Gabe in his new position behind her. "Do that again."

With a pronounced eye roll he did, saying as he walked through her, "Do you believe me now?"

She spun again to face him. "No. But I do believe I have some kind of residual brain damage from the other night—"

"Nat—Oh, sorry. Are you on the phone?" Jules whispered the last part, visibly looking for said phone.

"No." Natalie held up both hands to show there was no cell.

"You're not talking on Bluetooth?" Jules asked, pointing to her own ear.

"No."

Jules shook her head. "Then who were you talking to just now?"

Natalie shifted her gaze to Gabe whose raised eyebrows had a distinct I-told-you-so tilt to them.

"So you don't see a man standing in front of me. Or a whole bunch of other people all around us?" she asked.

"No," Jules answered slowly, drawing out the word.

Natalie drew in a breath, accepting the truth. "I definitely have to see a doctor."

An MRI should do it. Or a CT scan or whatever they used to look at brain damage.

With another deep frustrated groan, Gabe pivoted and strode directly through Jules.

The girl's body jolted.

She shivered, frowning. "What the hell? I just got this really weird chill. Almost like a low voltage shock."

That was exactly how Natalie felt when Gabe had walked through her.

Her heart pounding, breathing seemed to become harder as the evidence became impossible to ignore.

He said he was dead. He'd walked through her and through Jules. They'd both felt it.

What did that mean?

She wasn't dead, was she? She didn't think so, even if that interview had felt like a scene straight out of Hell.

So if she wasn't dead. But Gabe was. That meant...

Unable to draw air into her lungs, Natalie pressed one hand to her chest and bent at the waist to fight the wave of dizziness.

"Nat. You okay?"

"No."

"Do you need a doctor? I'll call 9-1-1. Ooo. Better yet, let me get that hottie doctor who brought you back to life."

As the Gen Z girl whipped out her ever-present cell

phone Natalie held up one hand to stop her. "No. Don't."

If she didn't want to end up in the psych ward at Binghamton General, she needed to figure this thing out before getting EMTs or the sheriff or anyone else with any authority and the ability to commit her involved.

And as for the hot doctor... She *really* didn't want that mean, rude, self-centered grump helping her with anything.

Straightening, she shot Ghost Gabe a glance and then focused on Jules. "I don't want you to panic, but I think I see dead people."

TWO WEEKS EARLIER

"Okay. One bottle of wine and one book. After the ten percent discount, that comes to thirty-one dollars and forty-three cents." Natalie pasted on a smile as the brunette handed over her credit card and reached for the canvas bag she'd brought in with her to carry her purchases.

Natalie hoped her smile said *thank you for shopping* and not *if more people don't start shopping here soon I'm going to have to sell and move back to the city.*

She used to be a happy person. Or at least she'd thought she'd been. The kind of person who smiled because she felt like it.

That had been back when she had health insurance and a steady paycheck and an annual bonus. When the company's bills and quarterly taxes were handled by the accounting department. Just as the other one-million and one things that running a business required had been handled by someone else. Some mysterious department on another floor of the Manhattan high rise.

Why had she left all that behind to buy a dilapidated old train depot in Mudville, New York and open a shop?

It had seemed like a good idea at the time, but at the moment she was having trouble remembering the reasons why.

Holding her tentative smile steady, Natalie ran the card and handed it back. "Here you go. Enjoy!"

"Guaranteed. Thanks so much." With what looked like genuine enthusiasm and a real smile, the woman grabbed the bag, turned, but then pivoted back.

The day's sole customer drew in a breath, as if she wanted to say something, but stopped herself as she let the air back out.

"Can I help you with something else?" Natalie asked.

A case of wine perhaps so I can pay the electric bill.

The woman hesitated again.

She was probably in her thirties, or maybe a young-looking forty-something. It was hard to tell. She wore sneakers, leggings and an oversized sweatshirt punctuated by a messy bun that captured her brown hair on top of her head, but Natalie couldn't pin down whether the outfit was for function or comfort.

Did she dress to be athletic or lazy? Hard to tell since the ensemble would work for either.

She'd been in before and was always pleasant enough. Friendly. Polite. She chose moderately priced wine—not the cheap stuff but not the most expensive either. And her book choices were all over the map, ranging from a stack of romance novels and an antique cookbook one week, to the new Jennifer Barnes *Hawthorne Brothers* Young Adult title the next.

Today she'd grabbed the new political thriller release from Jack Carr and had asked to preorder the next Cli Fi book coming from Marjorie B. Kellogg.

But this was the first time she ever seemed to want to offer more in the way of conversation than a passing comment on the weather.

"It's just, I had an idea," she began.

"All right." Natalie nodded.

Where was this going? Unlike her customer, Natalie had no ideas but since she had nothing else to do she was happy to listen.

Make that nothing else she *wanted* to do. There was still a ton on her To Do list that she'd been diligently ignoring. Owning a historic fixer-upper meant there was always something unpleasant to take care of.

"I hesitated to say anything until now—my fiancé

thinks I offer unsolicited advice too freely—but I really want you to succeed here." Her sincerity was palpable.

Natalie let out a short laugh. "I'd like that too, so advise away."

"Marketing is kind of my thing. So are books. And as you can see, I don't hate wine. But this town..." She shook her head. "It's hard to be the newcomer. To get a toe in the door. Trust me, I know. But if you can get them to open that door and let you in, these people will become your biggest supporters. They'll do anything for you."

"That sounds nice. But how do I do that? Get them to open the door." More importantly, get them inside her shop's door. And to open their wallets.

"That's where I might be able to help." She hesitated again then said, "I've got some ideas. If you're interested."

"I'm interested," Natalie blurted.

"Good. I'm Harper, by the way." Harper flashed her a smile and for the first time in a while, Natalie returned it with a genuine, heart-felt smile of her own as a glimmer of hope sparked to life inside her.

A quarter of an hour and zero customers later, Natalie was less hopeful but hiding that fact well. At least she assumed she was since Harper was still bubbling over with excitement and plans.

Natalie latched on to the latest idea. "Are book clubs even still a thing?" she asked.

Online, sure. On TV and in movies, definitely. But she didn't know anyone who belonged to an actual live and in-person book club.

"I really think it will work," Harper insisted. "The people in this town get together for any reason they can think of. I have to limit how many things I participate in or I'd be at a meeting every day of the week. Chamber. Rotary. Library Board. Zoning Board. Planning Board. Town Board. Fall Fest Planning Committee. Historical Society. Four Towns Community Yard Sale Day. The Ladies Amateur Detective Society..."

Harper stopped counting her list of meetings just as she ran out of fingers on both hands.

"That's a lot," Natalie agreed.

"Tell me about it." Harper snorted. "But what I'm saying is most locals don't think it's too much. And if you give them a compelling reason for one more excuse to meet, they'll jump on it."

"Okay. We can give it a try." She paused, her mind still spinning. "Have any ideas where to start?"

"I do." Harper glanced around at the empty shop. "Can you leave the register for a minute?"

Natalie stifled—mostly—her snort. "Yeah, I think I can safely leave for a minute."

On the off chance anyone actually came in, she locked the cash register, a vintage piece she'd splurged on back when she'd thought she'd have actual customers. She pocketed the key and moved around the counter to follow Harper, who was already reaching for the doorknob in the sidewall.

"Do you mind?" she asked.

"Uh, no. I mean, it's empty. And dirty." Natalie cringed at the state of the empty room she'd ignored until now.

"And it's the perfect meeting room," Harper said, walking inside and turning three-hundred and sixty degrees. "Would you feel comfortable offering it as a free meeting space to any local group who needed one?"

"Uh, yeah. I guess." Natalie looked around at the space, trying to see it with new eyes.

Instead of the dust and dirt, she focused on the details. The high ceilings. The large windows framed by thick molding. The exposed brick walls and wide wood floorboards.

The architecture had been what had won her heart in the first place. What had turned her Zillow window shopping into her quitting her job in HR in the city and becoming a store owner three hours north of Manhattan.

How could she pass on a historic, authentic, small town train depot for only twenty-four thousand dollars?

For less than the cost of renting her one room city apartment for a year, she'd have an actual yard. Small but with real live grass. She'd own a building with a place for her to both live and work. And she'd still have plenty of space left over for a community meeting room, apparently.

"By offering them the space for free, you'll get them in the door," Harper began.

"Where they might buy something," Natalie finished, starting to channel Harper's excitement.

Harper nodded. "Exactly."

Natalie evaluated the space. She could clean it up. Paint the ceiling to hide the stains and brighten up the room. That wouldn't cost too much if she did it herself. But there was another issue. "They're going to have to bring their own chairs though."

She couldn't justify the investment of buying dozens of chairs for a space that might only theoretically bring her some additional business.

Harper tipped her head. "They do that already for football games and concerts in the park, so it wouldn't be a problem. But I think I have a better idea."

The tinkling of the bell had Natalie jumping. "I gotta..."

"Go. I'm going to make a phone call."

Rushing to greet the newcomer, Natalie blew through the doorway only to find it was the mail person delivering—*oh, joy*—more bills.

She forced a smile. "Thank you. Have a nice day."

When the coast was clear, she let the scowl appear as she shoved the bills under the register. She couldn't deal with them now.

As she wondered if there was another sucker out there in the market for an old train depot in upstate New York, Harper reemerged.

She thrust her cell at Natalie. "What do you think?"

On the screen was what looked like a garage full of furniture. Old stuff, but not in horrible shape. An obnoxiously patterned sofa supported half a dozen mismatched wooden dining chairs stacked on top. Two comfy looking though worn armchairs flanked a small painted table.

"I'm not sure what I'm looking at," Natalie confessed.

"The furnishings for your new meeting space. And there's more than that if you're interested. My friend owns a thrift shop and does estate sales. She's looking to off load the big stuff. Free." Harper's brows rose as she waited for an answer.

Free was the magic word. Natalie took the cell and walked back to the empty room.

Amazingly, she no longer saw the cracked glass in one of the windowpanes or the thick layer of dust covering the scarred wood floor.

With the image of the furniture on the screen of the cell phone in her hand, she could envision various seating areas scattered around the room. One created by the sofa. Another by the two upholstered chairs and table.

After the addition of the dining chairs for more seating, she could picture book club members settling in for an evening of brisk literary discussion.

More than that, maybe this could become a quiet space where people could bring their newly purchased books and sit and read during the day.

Her heart was bursting with an excitement she hadn't felt since she'd first seen the pictures of the train station on Zillow.

And look how well that *had worked out...*

Shushing the negative voice in her head, she spun to face Harper, thrusting the cell toward her. "Yes."

"Yes to the furniture?" Harper asked taking her phone.

"Yes to everything. The community meetings. The book club. And especially the furniture."

In for a penny, in for a pound. If she was going down thanks to her Zillow habit and a fetish for old buildings at least she would go out not with a whimper but with a bang.

Speaking of banging... A vision of godly manliness strode past the first of the three windows in the meeting room.

Drawn like a magnet, Natalie moved closer and asked, "*Who* is that?"

He was tall. Tall enough she could clearly see his hard well-defined buns moving beneath his khaki pants above the window sill. She'd estimate he was over six feet of solid muscle. Muscle that strained the short sleeves of his black, collared shirt.

"Rumor has it he's a doctor. But you have to take Mudville gossip with a grain of salt. I've also heard from various sources that he's a private investigator, a Navy SEAL, and a serial killer. Take your pick. For the record, I do think the doctor theory has some legs to it."

She and Harper both tracked his progress as he moved past the second window. Once he'd passed the third and final window and was out of sight, Natalie could use her words and her brain again and asked, "Why do you think that—about the doctor theory?"

None of her doctors had ever looked like him.

"My friend who owns the bake shop was delivering an order to the lawyer who handled the lease on the warehouse next door to you. She said he was just leaving the office when she arrived and Dee called him Dr. Walsh as she said goodbye. Then, Dee told Bethany his first name is William. Jeez, listen to me. I sound as bad as one of the old biddies. Apparently gossip is contagious and I've been living in this town long enough to catch it."

Natalie didn't mind a little gossip, especially if it entailed a certain tall, dark and handsome doctor. But she still had more questions. "What does a doctor want with a warehouse?"

"Maybe he's opening a clinic or something?" Harper shrugged.

Natalie cringed. "Seems like it would take a lot of work to turn that building into anything, but especially a sterile facility."

After the last month, she considered herself well qualified as an expert in old buildings and what it took to fix them up. The old warehouse next door looked like a case of tetanus waiting to happen. And that was only if it didn't collapse on him first.

"At least it will improve your view if he fixes it up. And your property value too."

She was all for increased property values just in case

Harper's book club plan didn't work. Fingers crossed it would work and she and Once Upon a Vine would be here next to the new hot neighbor for a good long time.

Chapter Three

Longingly staring at the list of shows she wanted to watch on Netflix, Natalie tried to narrow it down to just one for tonight. She'd never be able to get through the whole list before she canceled her subscription at the end of the month.

Pinching pennies sucked.

On the coffee table, her phone rang, reminding her she should look into a cheaper cellular plan.

Harper's name appeared on the display.

It had only been a few hours since Harper had left the shop with a spring in her step. She'd gone on her merry way with Natalie's blessing—carte blanche to do whatever she thought would help get people into the shop.

Maybe she had good news about the book club.

Swapping the remote control for the cell, Natalie answered, "Hello."

"What are you doing right now?" Harper asked, excitement in her voice.

There was no way Natalie was going to admit she was already in her pajamas just fifteen minutes after locking the shop door at six. Or that she was about to microwave a frozen meal from the dollar store.

"Uh, nothing. Why?"

"You have to come to the Muddy River Inn. Right now."

Having a friend would be nice. More than one, even nicer. But there was no way she could justify the expense of a night out on the town with Harper right now.

Putting on her happy, *I'm not pitiful at all* voice, she said, "Aw, thanks. But I'm really beat from work today."

"We'll have you home early. I promise."

As she wondered who *we* was, she was about to continue begging out of the date when Harper continued.

"Hot doctor slash serial killer is here."

That stopped the excuse that was right on the tip of Natalie's tongue. "He is?"

"He is, and he's even hotter close up. Come on. I want you to meet my friends and they're dying to meet you too. I insist you let me treat you to a welcome to Mudville girls' night out."

"How can I say no to that?" Natalie glanced down at her current outfit. "Um, give me fifteen minutes and I'll meet you there."

"Perfect. Hot doc just ordered food."

Even as a newcomer she knew where the bar was, but she'd never braved going inside. It had felt too daunting to walk in and then sit there by herself.

Meeting Harper and her friends solved the problem of sitting alone but not the fear of walking through the door as it seemed like every eye in the place turned toward her.

"Natalie!" Harper stood and waved from a table where two other women sat.

She smiled with relief and had started toward them when her gaze hit on hot doctor, sitting alone not too far from them. Even if Natalie hadn't noticed him already, she would have after Harper waggled her eyebrows while tipping her head toward him and pointing.

He was even better looking up close... and distracting. As he sat scrolling through his cell, she bumped one hip into the corner of a table, making the little vase wobble but not fall over.

She forced herself to focus.

Trying not to trip over her own feet she wove her

way between tables, chairs and patrons and finally made it to the table of women.

Relieved that they too were dressed casually in jeans like she was, she smiled. "Hi. Thanks for inviting me."

"Of course." Harper waved away her thanks. "Natalie, this is Red who owns Red's Resale and Bethany who owns Honey Buns, the bakery."

The women greeted her like they were old friends.

"What do you want to drink?" Harper asked.

"We haven't ordered food yet. Here's a menu," Bethany offered.

"The garlic parmesan hot wings are amazeballs," Red added.

"Um…" A tad overwhelmed Natalie forced herself to focus. That was impossible so with one look at the three matching margarita glasses in front of her companions, she said, "I'll have one of those."

"Good choice. I'll tell the bartender." As Harper jumped up, Natalie took the time to glance around her.

"This place is adorable," she said.

Dive bar on the outside, it was a surprise of quirky mismatched furnishings on the inside.

Red nodded. "Right? I bet your shop's adorable too. Harper told me you want the furniture."

"Is that from you?" Natalie asked.

"Yes, ma'am. I'm happy to get rid of it."

"I don't know how to thank you, but I thought maybe I can print out a little sign and put it in a nice frame that says something like *furnishings provided by Red's Resale*. If that's all right with you."

"Thanks. That would be great." Red smiled.

"Hot doctor's drinking lemonade," Harper reported as she planted an icy margarita glass in front of Natalie.

"Thank you. And maybe he's on call or something," Natalie suggested, keeping her voice low.

"He's built more like he's a trainer at a gym. Maybe he's like a physical therapist?" Red suggested.

"Maybe." Bethany said low. "But Alice Mudd insists he's a murderer."

"Not just a murderer. *Serial killer*," Harper corrected. "Although Jack the Ripper was supposed to be a doctor too so…"

"Well, since we're listing all the gossip, old Buck said he heard he's a mercenary for hire," Bethany added.

Taking a sip of her drink, Red held up one finger, swallowed then said, "Actually, Jeb told Cash he heard he was a hit man."

Harper bobbed her head side to side. "Mercenary. Hit man. Both killers for hire so that's kind of close. Could be something to that one. And Mrs. Trout told Agnes she saw bodies—plural—being carried into the warehouse."

"So he's a serial killer who keeps his victims' bodies?" Red asked. "That doesn't seem very smart."

"Dahmer did that," Natalie informed them. That was one show Natalie had gotten to binge before she became cash strapped.

In hindsight, since she'd have to cancel Netflix soon, she probably should have chosen better. A rewatch of Bridgerton season one would have been more pleasant.

From where she sat, Natalie could see the probable physician-possible psychopath's profile.

Good strong chin. Great cheekbones. An amazing head of thick, dark hair, long enough to fall over his forehead and give him a rakish look, but not so long it hit the collar of his shirt at the back of his neck.

She wondered what color his eyes were as he stabbed a piece of lettuce in his salad with a fork that looked small while gripped in his big strong hands.

Interesting choice. Salad and lemonade. Pretty much the opposite of her own order of a margarita with Butter Garlic Parmesan Wings.

"Considering how hot he is, is it wrong I'm considering if being a possible serial killer is a deal breaker or not?" Natalie asked, her tongue feeling loose thanks to the drink.

"No. I'd be asking myself the same question if I wasn't with Cash," Red said.

"We'd *all* be asking ourselves that question if we weren't taken women," Harper clarified.

Bethany nodded in agreement as she sucked on her straw and all four of them stared at him eating.

"I say go introduce yourself," Harper said. "You are his neighbor. You've got an automatic in."

"And say what? Hey, I own the building next to yours. Wanna show me your collection of bodies sometime?"

"I might not lead with the bodies, but the rest works." Red shrugged.

While they talked, hot doctor had downed the last of his lemonade and tossed a twenty-dollar bill on the table where he'd abandoned the last of the lettuce in the bowl. He stood and they got the full impact of the length and breadth of his hot body.

He turned toward them and Natalie couldn't breathe. Why was he coming this way?

As he walked straight at her she caught the orange glow of an EXIT sign in her peripheral vision and realized there was a door behind them in addition to the front door she'd entered through.

Their table was silent as all four were glued to his every move. And that was before he tipped his head toward them and said in a deep rich voice that sent a tingle down her spine and all the way to her nether region, "Ladies."

Something inside Natalie snapped. Whether it was the tequila or his testosterone, she forgot she was shy and blurted, "Hi-I'm-your-neighbor-I-own-the-train-depot."

At that, his gaze pinned her where she sat trembling as he asked, "What's your name?"

Heart pounding, she answered, "Nat—Natalie."

He bent low. Close. She saw his eyes were green and amazing and she wanted to stare into them for the rest of her life. Or at least for an hour or so tonight. Preferably while in her bed.

"Well, Natalie. It's rude to stare and talk about people while they're trying to eat dinner."

Straightening he swept a glance over all four of them seated at the table.

"Have a good night, ladies." With that, he pushed the door open with a shove and left the building.

"That went well," Red commented flatly.

Natalie used both hands to cover her face—in particular her burning cheeks. "Oh my God. I'll never be able to face him again."

Harper patted her shoulder. "You're going to have to, sweetie. He's your neighbor."

"I know," Natalie groaned. "Don't remind me."

Her only hope now was that he really was a serial

killer—or a Navy SEAL, mercenary or hitman—and would have to leave town for one of his jobs.

As misery and shame overwhelmed Natalie and she made plans to buy curtains to hang on his side of the building until she could sell the place, Red lifted one hand and called toward the bar, "We're going to need another round here."

Chapter Four

NATALIE CONSIDERED HERSELF A FAIRLY intelligent individual. Case in point, she'd recently learned to be careful what she wished for.

As her head spun she knew it was a lesson she'd never forget.

Boxes of books to fill special book club orders were stacked and waiting to be unpacked right where the delivery person had left them yesterday.

The shop's meeting room sign-up was filling so fast she'd resorted to buying a big paper calendar to hang next to the register because it was faster to scribble in a commitment than to log into her online calendar.

Customers streamed in steadily from opening until closing, which meant fitting in time to eat, and to pee, was challenging. And all it had taken was two weeks of implementing Harper's plan.

One upside to being this busy was she hadn't even seen hot rude doctor since that night.

Thank goodness for that. She had enough stress in her life. She didn't need to be lectured on manners again by a possible murdering medical maniac. Particularly now while she was trying to power through the day on only the single cup of coffee she'd consumed before unlocking the door.

She needed help, which was a problem for a couple of reasons.

First, money was finally coming in but it was going out just as fast with all the stock she'd been ordering. After paying bills there didn't seem to be enough left over to spend on the luxury of staff.

Second, who would she even hire?

The older retired crowd who shopped here didn't seem likely to want to work part time for minimum wage. The slightly younger demographic who ran in after work to quickly grab a bottle of wine for dinner seemed to have money but no time. So again, they weren't candidates for a part-timer.

She'd make it work on her own. Somehow. Starting with opening the damn boxes of books so she could call

all those who'd placed the special orders to come pick them up.

Armed with a box cutter, she reached for the box on the top of the stack.

The bell above the door—the one she was considering ripping down if she could just get a second to drag over a chair so she could reach it—tinkled yet again, setting her nerves on edge.

Drawing in a deep breath she resigned herself to the interruption.

It would be fine. She'd lock up tonight at closing time, microwave something quick to eat and unpack everything when she could make her phone calls in peace. Multitasking was overrated anyway.

Resting the box cutter on the register counter, she turned and smiled when she saw her ad hoc marketing and business advisor striding toward her.

"Good morning. I brought you coffee and a sweet from Honey Buns." Harper thrust both hands forward, one containing a paper cup and one a brown paper bag.

"Bless you," Natalie said, gratefully taking both from her new friend.

She'd deal with the issue of having to pee later in exchange for a caffeine boost now.

Harper's eyes lit as her gaze hit upon the boxes. "Books?"

"Yes. Lots of them."

"Can we open them?" she asked with a mixture of excitement and hesitation, looking like a kid facing a towering stack of wrapped presents on Christmas morning.

Natalie laughed, putting down the bag to pick up the box cutter. She handed it to Harper. "Be my guest."

"Yay!" Harper squealed. "I love book deliveries."

"Well, I've got plenty of them. Have at it. You're welcome to get your book unboxing fix anytime you want."

"Seriously? I'd love that."

Natalie had been joking but hell, why not? "Um, yeah. Of course. Thanks. I could use the extra pair of hands."

"Can I put the unboxing on my TikTok?" Harper asked.

"Um, sure."

"Great. I'll tag you."

"I'm ready to check out." A woman struggling to carry one toddler, two children's books and three bottles of wine loaded her purchases onto the counter, saving Natalie from having to confess to Harper she hadn't yet set up a TikTok to tag.

One thing at a time.

She indulged in a big swallow of coffee as she made her way back to the counter and the customer.

Looking longingly at the brown paper bag containing the treat she hadn't gotten to even glance at yet, she shoved that on the shelf below the counter and began ringing up the items.

By the time the vocal child and the stressed-out mother were out the door, Harper had all three boxes cut open and the contents of the first one stacked in two neat piles on the end of the counter.

Harper paused next to the tower of books. "I wasn't sure if these are for store stock or a special order for the book club."

There were two book clubs so far. One for steamy romance and one for cozy mystery. But Harper had plans for more, including one for thrillers and suspense and one for historical romance.

And with the first book the club picked for their inaugural meeting came the special orders. One or two chose to read on their eReaders, but most wanted the paperback. And to accommodate those readers and keep them from ordering from Amazon, Natalie offered a twenty-percent discount on any book club purchases.

It worked. Yes, it cut severely into her profit margin, but a hundred percent of nothing was nothing. She'd rather cut the price and keep the sale.

But along with the special orders came the need to notify each and every one of the book club members.

"Book club, mostly," she said in answer to Harper's question as she reached for her list. "I guess I'd better get started on all these phone calls."

"Can I see the list?" Harper held out her hand for the paper, which Natalie happily handed over. "I can take care of this for you with two phone calls. Alice Mudd will make sure all the cozy mystery club members get the message. And I saw the romance club's title in that other box. I'll text my Aunt Agnes. She has the romance book club already set up for an email blast."

Natalie let out a breathy laugh. "That would be a huge help." She might actually have time to pee sometime today.

Harper paused, tipping her head to one side. "Do you need help?"

"Yes," Natalie answered without hesitation.

"Would you consider a student?" Harper asked.

She hadn't thought of that but why not? "Sure."

"I know someone. She's young but she's smart and she'll work cheap."

"Cheap is good." Natalie nodded.

"I'll call—Jesus. What was that?" Harper pressed one hand to her chest as a black blur whizzed past.

Natalie watched as it leapt onto the windowsill. "That's the cat."

"Aw, I love when bookstores have cats. I didn't know you had one." Hand extended, Harper moved slowly toward the window.

The bastard cat, who never let Natalie pet him even once but had no problem eating the food she finally bought for him, let Harper scratch his head. He even looked like he enjoyed it.

"I don't have one. He showed up one day and now he thinks he lives here. I find him asleep on top of the bookshelves every morning when I open. He's getting in and out but I can't figure out how." She hated to think there was a cat sized hole somewhere in her building she had yet to find.

"Then let's make him earn his keep." She whipped out her cell and snapped a picture as the damn cat lifted his head in the sunlight and stared right at the camera, as if he were posing. Like some sort of feline GQ model. "What's his name? I'll post this on my Insta and tag you."

"I haven't named him yet."

Harper came back to where Natalie stood with a mouthful of honey bun and rested an elbow on the counter. "Something literary, I think. Hmm..."

The cat jumped down off the windowsill and ran

across the store. He leapt on to the counter and rubbed his head on Harper's chin as she laughed.

Natalie shook her head. "He acts like a stuck-up snob with me, giving me the cold shoulder. Even though I'm the one who feeds you, you know." She directed that last part at the cat, who ignored her as he purred and serpentined his body against Harper.

"A stuck-up snob, huh? I think it's clear. He's Mr. Darcy."

"That's perfect." In fact, maybe the cat belonged to the snooty hot doctor. If so, it should go home so they could judge her together from their warehouse full of bodies.

Speaking of...

"Did you hear anything more about Doctor Death?" she asked.

Harper nodded. "Mary Brimley is insisting she saw another body being delivered in a pick-up truck and carried inside in a body bag this week."

Natalie frowned. "What could he be hoarding in there that looks like dead bodies? CPR dummies, maybe?"

Harper shrugged. "No clue. I'm torn between being annoyed I don't know the truth and happy that the mystery is keeping all the old biddies occupied and out of my personal life."

Natalie laughed. "They can't be that bad."

Shooting a stare at her from beneath raised brows, Harper said, "Oh, sweetie, you have no idea."

She visibly shook then gathered herself and with one last pat on the cat's head she whipped out her phone again.

"Okay, so I posted Mr. Darcy's bookstore debut. I'm texting my Aunt Agnes now. She can call Alice and then email the club members so you can get rid of these books… and I'll text your potential new employee. Can I tell her she can come in anytime the shop's open to meet with you?" Harper raised her gaze briefly from her cell.

"Sure. Thank you."

She waved away the thanks. "No problem. Happy to help."

Fingers flying, Harper fired off the texts. It would be easy to forget Harper was a professional writer since she seemed to be so busy with everything else besides writing.

Meanwhile Natalie was barely managing to juggle the pastry and the coffee. Especially since the cat insisted on using her counter for a bed.

"All right. Done. Now I guess I should get back home and get some work done. That book's not going to write itself." A text chimed on Harper's phone while it was still in her hand. She frowned as she read it, then let out a groan.

"Is everything okay?" Natalie asked.

"Yeah." She rolled her eyes. "Stone wants me to get home before the big storm hits."

"Storm? I didn't hear anything about that." Natalie glanced outside.

It had been sunny all morning. Although the sky did seem to have taken on an ominous greenish tinge in the past few minutes.

"One of the hazards of being engaged to a farmer. They're way too attuned to the weather." She typed something into her phone then shoved the cell into her pocket. "All right. I'm off. I don't want to give Stone a reason to say *I told you so*. He's smug enough already as it is. Stay safe in this supposed big storm. You too, Mr. Darcy."

Harper kissed the cat on the top of the head and he looked happy as a clam to receive the attention.

Shaking her head as she resigned herself to the fact the cat liked Harper better than her, Natalie said, "We'll be safe. I promise."

She didn't go outside much when the weather was nice. She couldn't imagine any reason why she'd be tempted to go outside in a storm.

Chapter Five

"What the heck?" Natalie stared out the window in disbelief.

Not an hour after Harper had left the shop on the heels of her fiancé's storm warning, the skies had opened up. If it wasn't actually hail, it was the hardest rain Natalie had ever heard and the largest drops she'd ever seen.

And right in the middle of the storm what did she see out the window but that damn cat.

Of all the times she'd found him lounging inside the store on a beautiful day, Mr. Darcy chose now to go outside. In the middle of a typhoon.

He was hunkered down under the dumpster that had been dropped off at hot mean doctor's warehouse, but by how the cat looked more like a drowned rat, the large metal container wasn't offering much in the way of shelter from the storm.

"Dammit."

She knew what she had to do even if it was the last thing she wanted to. She was going to have to brave the storm and try to get that dumb cat inside.

"Not even my cat. Just because Harper named him doesn't mean I should have to go out in a storm to get him. Shouldn't a cat be smart enough to come in from the rain anyway? What the hell?" The steady stream of grumbling, accompanied by what was admittedly childish stomping on her part as she went upstairs to get a raincoat, made her feel moderately better.

She might have stomped and pouted all the way to the dumpster where the cat hunkered down and glared at her like she was an axe murdering stranger rather than his rescuer.

"Seriously? After I've been buying you the good cans of food instead of the cheap no name dry stuff?" With what might have been a growl, she bent and tried to grab the cat, who effectively avoided her by backing up farther beneath the dumpster.

"I'm going to leave you there if you don't come out."

A very uncatlike whine caught her attention over the noise of the rain pummeling her and the dumpster. It sounded almost like a... dog?

She bent at the waist and hanging her head upside down braved Mr. Darcy's very rude hiss to peer beneath the dumpster. And there it was, a tiny shivering whimpering body half the size of Mr. Darcy but most definitely a dog.

"What are you doing under there? Will you come out and let me pick you up? I won't hurt you."

Apparently she didn't speak animal well. At least not convincingly. Mr. Darcy took off for the shop, sprinting like he'd been shot out of a cannon. On his heels but moving much more slowly on his stubby little legs, was the dog.

That left Natalie standing alone next to a dumpster in the torrential rain and looking like an idiot. And of course, mean hot doctor chose that moment to come out of the door of the warehouse.

"What are you doing here?" he asked with about as much charm as she'd come to expect from him. That being none.

"Nothing," she said, immediately on defense against the accusation in his voice.

He was looking at her as if she were some sort of stalker going through his garbage so she figured she'd better explain.

"I was trying to save a dog and cat from the storm. Are they yours?" she yelled to be heard over the rain.

On a snort, he said, "God no. The last thing I need is a pet."

"That figures," she mumbled, then added much louder, "Pleasure talking to you, as always," she said with what she hoped was obvious sarcasm, although some of that might have been lost to the noise of the storm.

Dripping and miserable she spun on squishy feet in soaked sneakers and strode back toward her shop.

The order of the following events jumbled together as the world around her seemed to explode.

There was a loud *crack*. Then a *boom* accompanied by sparks falling from overhead.

It was all enough to have her pouring on the speed to get back inside.

She was so wet already she didn't even think twice about running directly through the ankle-deep puddle between her and the shop.

As she ran she barely heard—and definitely ignored—crabby doctor's shout just before her body exploded in intense tingling pain. She was paralyzed and convulsing at the same time. Unable to move but also incapable of remaining still.

And just as what felt like a truck crashed into her back, knocking her over, the world went blissfully black.

She awoke sometime later—she had no idea how much later—to what could only be described as pandemonium. The rain had let up and was barely a drizzle, but everything else was like hell had broken loose.

A fire whistle blared and there were flashing lights emitting from multiple vehicles, one of which seemed to be a utility truck. With the vehicles came what seemed like an inordinately large number of workers.

Even grumpy doctor was there, off to the side. It looked like he was being interviewed by a man in a uniform.

Hovering over her, EMTs surrounded her where she lay on the wet ground.

And, strangest of all, there was one freckled young girl who leaned low and said, "Oh my God. Are you okay? You were like legit dead."

"Wh—who are you?" Natalie managed in a weak voice as she realized that everything hurt.

"I'm Julia, but everyone calls me Jules. Harper said to come by the shop for a job interview."

The shop. She'd left the door unlocked. And the money was still in the register. She needed to get back inside.

It was then she realized she was strapped to a board and being lifted into the air and she panicked.

"Can you lock the shop door?" she managed to shout as they bounced her toward the open ambulance. Whether the young stranger heard her before the EMTs slid her inside and slammed the double doors was unclear.

One day, probably in therapy if she could ever afford it sometime in the future, she'd have to explore that on the heels of almost dying she was most concerned about the shop getting robbed.

Sole entrepreneurship was a demanding bitch.

Chapter Six

"I'M REALLY FINE," NATALIE SAID FOR WHAT had to be the tenth time that hour.

Fine except for the sick feeling caused by her calculating what her insurance deductible for the ambulance and Emergency Room visit was going to cost. That made her feel more than a little ill.

The nurse, dressed in colorfully patterned scrubs, had stopped explaining all the horrifying things that happened to a body during electrocution and had moved on to just nodding and grunting in acknowledgment of Natalie's protests about not being released yet.

"Knock-knock." At the sound of Harper's voice, Natalie whipped her gaze to the door.

She felt a wave of relief. They hadn't been friends long but after being surrounded by strangers for she didn't know how many hours, Natalie was grateful for a familiar face.

"Hi." That was all she could get out as her gratitude started to manifest itself in tears that she choked back.

"How is she?" Harper asked the nurse directly.

"She's lucky, is what she is." The nurse shot her a glance then headed out the door leaving Natalie alone with Harper.

"I think she's tired of my saying I'm fine and I want to get out of here," Natalie whispered.

Harper leaned close. "I don't blame you." Then she smiled. "But seriously. Don't worry. We've got the shop covered."

There was that mysterious *we* again that Harper liked to throw around. "We?"

"Jules—the high school girl I suggested you hire— called me when the ambulance took you away so I came right over. We locked up the shop and put a sign in the window explaining the early closing. But people kept showing up to pick up their book club orders and since you said they were all prepaid, I left Jules there with the list of who'd preordered. When I left she was making them give her their name and the book title before she'd unlock the door and hand them the book."

Natalie cringed. "Oh, no. They must *love* that."

Harper lifted one shoulder. "Actually, they're loving

it. Alice Mudd said it reminded her of the stories her father used to tell her about the speakeasies during Prohibition. It might be a good theme for a promotion. Whisper the secret codeword at the register and get ten percent off your order. Something like that."

Even in a hospital surrounded by beeping machines and moaning patients, Harper was still on her marketing game.

Natalie laughed. "I like it. Remind me later in case frying my brain has cost me my short-term memory."

"I will." Harper smiled then sobered. "How are you really?"

"Fine. Really. I just want to be home." Or at least at the train depot, which was as close to a home as she had right now.

"We're pulling as many strings as we can to get you out of here," Harper promised.

Again with the *we*...

"I stopped by the front desk and talked to the head nurse or administrator or whoever she is. I promised that when you're released, I'd stay with you so you wouldn't be alone. That's one thing they worry about when releasing a patient. And Jules's older sister is a nursing student at Delhi so she's done some training in this hospital and has some contacts. She's been trying to get whatever information she can."

The hope that she'd get out of there soon with all these people pulling for her was interrupted as Harper added, "Oh, and she's taking care of your dog for you. How did I not know you had a dog?"

As a memory shot through the jumbled haze of the past few hours, Natalie's eyes flew wide. *The dog.*

She covered her face with both hands and groaned. "I don't."

Just like she didn't used to have a cat. It looked as if she might have both now.

"He just showed up along with the cat," she continued.

Harper lifted a brow. "All right. Don't worry about it. We'll figure out who he belongs to. A really nice woman runs the animal shelter. She'll help us. But for now, Jules is taking care of him at the shop."

Jules was proving herself invaluable.

"I guess I have a new employee." The weight of that new financial burden added to her already stretched budget pressed heavily upon her.

"I told you she was smart and capable."

"Mm-hm. You did." Natalie could only hope she also worked for cheap, as promised.

"She's also a whizz with technology and social media. The girl lives on her phone. In fact, she sent me this." Harper turned her cell phone to face Natalie.

On the screen she could just make out two forms through the rain. One, lying flat out on the ground while wearing a yellow rain slicker that looked suspiciously like her own. The second, kneeling above the first, appeared to be performing CPR.

Natalie swallowed hard. "Is this—"

"You and the hot doc," Harper confirmed.

Heart clenched, Natalie asked, "How long did he—how long did it take?"

"Over three minutes, according to the video."

Those minutes seemed an eternity as Natalie watched him relentlessly, tirelessly, pump her chest, manually forcing her heart to work. Long enough that the rain slowed. So long that Jules had moved outside to get a closer shot.

At one point he leaned back on his heels, felt for a pulse then glanced up at the camera with a heartbreakingly handsome, devastated expression worthy of any A-list Hollywood actor.

She saw the determination and a shadow of something else—anger maybe—cross his face.

That was when he fisted one hand and, focusing on her lifeless body lying prone beneath him on the ground, punched her in the chest hard, just once.

He checked for a pulse again and this time, his eyes

closed as he drew in a deep chest expanding breath then let it out.

When he opened his eyes again, it was to look directly at the camera—or more likely at Jules—as he said on a breath, "She's alive."

At least now she knew why her chest felt so sore.

But she had a feeling it was this man who'd caused this newly onset symptom—a tight yearning in her now racing heart. Because he did something amazing next.

He smiled. *Actually* smiled. And the effect was devastating.

Hot doc wasn't just handsome. He was ethereal. Godlike in his gorgeousness. Splendidly, sinfully sexy. Magnificently manly. Powerful in his prowess.

He was a literal heartthrob, as in her own heart pounded harder just from the video of this man. The man who'd forced her stalled heart to beat once again.

Seeing all of that alpha male energy focused solely on her in the video did one other thing.

It made her want that again. Him solely focused on her. On her body...just without the being dead part.

The nurse returned, interrupting her sexual fantasies about her savior to say, "You ready to go home?"

"Yes," Natalie burst out with feeling.

She had a hot doc to thank.

Chapter Seven

"So the dog really just showed up here?" Jules, Once Upon a Vines' new eighteen-year-old, part time employee, asked.

"He did." Natalie nodded and felt the stiffness in her neck and shoulders.

Her whole body was sore. It felt as if she'd done a super hard workout at the gym. Unfortunately, her muscle aches were caused by electrocution and not her enthusiasm for working out—which didn't exist.

"You think he's a stray?" Jules rubbed the dog's snout which sent his whole body into a tail-wagging wiggle.

"I don't know much about chihuahuas, but he looks like a purebred. Maybe he's just lost or ran away,"

Harper suggested while dutifully giving Mr. Darcy all the petting he demanded from her.

"He's tiny but he does look healthy. Like he's been well-cared for," Natalie agreed.

"No collar though," Jules observed.

Natalie let out a sniff. "His head's so small maybe he slipped out of it."

Next to Mr. Darcy, the surprisingly large black cat, the little white chihuahua looked like a toy.

"I'll text Stephanie—she runs the animal shelter—and ask if anyone reported a missing dog. She can put a pic of this little guy on the shelter's socials too," Jules offered.

Natalie pouted. "I don't want him to go to a shelter, but I just don't think I have the bandwidth for a dog right now. The cat is one thing. He comes and goes as he pleases. But a dog needs to be walked..."

"No worries." Jules ruffled the dog's head. "I'll take the little guy home with me until we find the owner."

"Are you sure your parents won't mind?" Natalie asked.

The girl shook her head. "Won't mind at all. I promise."

Natalie wasn't sure she believed that but it was easier to just agree. She had too many other things on her mind.

"And he was hiding under the dumpster in that storm?" Harper asked.

Natalie nodded. "Along with Mr. Darcy, which was the reason I went outside in the first place."

"Which led to your epic meet cute with Doctor Hottie." Jules grinned.

Meet cutes didn't usually entail one of the parties being dead, even temporarily.

Natalie lifted a brow. "Not sure I'd call it a meet cute." Or epic—his bringing her back from the dead notwithstanding.

"I would." Harper grinned.

"There he is," Jules hissed, even though the *he* in question was outside, yards away, and wouldn't be able to hear them speaking about him—again.

Natalie followed Jules's gaze out the shop's window and saw hot doc was indeed walking toward the warehouse.

"I should probably say thank you to him, right?" Natalie turned to ask Jules and Harper for their opinion.

"Heck, yeah, you should." Jules nodded.

"I agree. Go." Harper spun Natalie toward the door. "Quick before he gets away."

He was about to go inside the warehouse, which wouldn't exactly be *getting away,* but she wouldn't feel comfortable knocking on the door of the mysterious and decrepit building in an attempt to chase him down just to say thank you.

"Okay. I'm going."

Abandoning the shop and whatever customers might come in to Jules and Harper's care, Natalie took off in a jog, weaving between display tables and shelving until she reached the door.

She yanked it open, sending the bell above jangling wildly. She trotted across the distance between his building and hers, cautiously leaping over the puddle still there even though the downed power line had long since been repaired.

As he was just a couple of steps from the warehouse door, she panicked.

What was hot doc's name? She couldn't remember so she called, "Um, hey! Wait up a second."

He did, stopping in his path to turn slowly and level a stare upon her as she ran toward him.

She was embarrassingly out of breath when she finally reached where he stood.

One dark brow quirked up as he said, "Yes?"

"I, uh, wanted to thank you for... you know." She gestured toward the nearby standing water with the flip of one wrist.

"Bringing you back to life after you ran into a puddle

with a live wire in it even though I yelled for you to stop?" he asked.

Her face heated. "Yeah. That."

"Don't worry about it." He turned to go.

That was it?

"Wait." She grabbed his forearm and—holy hell did he have some muscles on him.

He glanced down at where she held him, even though her fingers didn't come near to wrapping around the full girth of his arm.

The fire in her cheeks intensified as she wondered what else on him might be girthy—

She dropped her hold on his massive muscles. "I, um, wanted to thank you properly."

"You've already done that."

"But can't I—I don't know—buy you a drink or something?" She had a vague memory of him not drinking at the bar and quickly added, "Or lemonade or coffee or—"

"I'd prefer if you didn't buy me anything and just let me get back to work. I have a lot to do."

Her cheeks burned now for a different reason. Embarrassment. Shame. Anger. It all swirled into a pulse pounding internal cacophony of emotion caused by this man.

What the hell? How could a person be so rude in the face of someone offering to do something nice for them?

She frowned and lifted her chin to glare up at him—darn, he was tall. "Oh, you can get back to work. I won't be bothering you again."

"Thank you." He said it in a flat, matter of fact tone, completely devoid of attitude. Without heat. Just cold, calm words as he turned away.

He tugged open the warehouse door with a groan and a squeak—the door, not him—and then closed it behind him with a definitive slam.

Left reeling in his wake, Natalie grumbled all the way back to the shop. She'd barely cleared the doorway when Harper and Jules, virtually bubbling over in their quest for information, attacked her.

"How did it go? What did he say?" Harper asked.

"We tried reading hot doctor's lips but it didn't work," Jules added.

"Shh." Natalie glanced around to see if there were any customers nearby to hear them. "And it went horribly. I hate to break it to you both, but hot doctor is a rude, obnoxious, horrible man. Even if he did save my life."

Some people just weren't fit to live in polite society. Hot doctor was obviously one of them.

What a shame all those good genes were wasted on him. Great hair. Incredible body. Amazing eyes. The packaging was perfection. But inside? Things were not so good. And why couldn't she remember his name? It must be the effects of the electricity. A frightening one she hoped didn't last.

Pawing through her memories she flashed back to all the past discussions about hot doc. There were too many considering what a dick he was. William Wallace? No. That was Mel Gibson's character in *Braveheart*. There was a W though...

Walsh. Doctor Walsh. That was it. William Walsh.

Phew. No brain damage after all. Thank God.

Meanwhile, Jules looked crestfallen as her lips formed a pout and her brows drew low. "Oh, no. I hate he's not as nice on the inside as he is on the outside."

Harper, on the other hand, simply appeared resigned. She pressed her lips tightly together and breathed out a loud breath. "Oh, well. That's a shame," she said.

"It really is." Natalie nodded in agreement.

They all took a moment to mourn the death of the fantasy of what might have been between her and hot doc, then Natalie dragged herself back to work mode. "So, tonight..."

"Tonight." Harper nodded. "You have triple R's very first meeting."

"Triple R?" Natalie asked, confused.

"They gave themselves that name while you were in the hospital. The Raunchy Romance Readers Book Club," Harper elaborated.

Natalie's brow furrowed. "*That's* what they want to call themselves?"

"Right?" Jules agreed. "That's what I said."

Harper shrugged. "My aunt said they're tired of being shamed for reading romance novels and it was time to unapologetically proclaim their love of the genre. Hmm... That might be a good line to use for promotion."

"On it." Jules whipped out her phone.

"Good. So anyway, Agnes asked if it would be all right if they brought in refreshments. I believe it's iced tea and cookies. They'd bring cups and napkins and everything they'll need. I said yes. I hope that's okay." Harper cringed.

"Whatever they want to bring in is fine." Natalie waved away her concern.

Although that brought up one thing she'd been meaning to do. Buy a trash can. She'd been making do with a garbage bag, sans can. But the variety slash hardware store down the block had some. Metal. Plastic. Big. Small. She'd noticed them last time she'd been there buying paint to spruce up the meeting room.

And actually, the store had cheap wine glasses too. Perhaps if she supplied a dozen wine glasses or so and a corkscrew, casually placed on a side table in the meeting room, it might encourage the groups meeting there to buy a few bottles of wine to enjoy during their meeting.

Excited now, Natalie asked, "Would you two mind watching the shop for five minutes while I run to the hardware store?"

"No problem. You know I love playing shopkeeper." Harper smiled.

"I know you do." Natalie laughed. "Okay, back in a few."

She grabbed her wallet and hustled out the door and toward the shop that, typical of a small-town Main Street store, sold everything from greeting cards to electrical and plumbing supplies.

Also typical of a small town, everything was right there on Main Street, clustered together. On the way to the village variety store, she passed the pharmacy, the community center, the architecturally beautiful historic church and its attached and even older cemetery.

For some reason, the cemetery was exceptionally active today. The one time she'd walked through she'd noticed gravestones from as far back as the Revolutionary War. She hadn't thought it was still a working cemetery, as in there were no modern-day internments, but it was teeming with visitors today.

Maybe there was some sort of historical society tour going on.

With a brief regret that she couldn't participate, she headed into the store.

Inside she found exactly what she needed. Boxed wine glasses. A dozen for nine bucks. She grabbed two and then a sturdy good-sized trash can. That cost more than both boxes of wine glasses added together, which stung since she'd get far less enjoyment and no additional wine sales from the trash can.

She probably should have taken the car rather than walking but she managed to fit the two boxes inside the trash can and make her way up to the cash register.

As the clerk rang up her purchases, she asked, "What's going on over at the cemetery today?"

"The cemetery?" The man, whose name tag pronounced him as Frank, shrugged. "Nothing as far as I know."

"There's a bunch of people walking around. I thought maybe it was a tour or something."

He shook his head and glanced toward the front of the store where an employee was pricing a box of mosquito repellent. "Chris! You know of anything happening over at the cemetery today?"

"Nope."

"This lady says there's a bunch of people over there doing something."

Chris leaned to peer through the large front windows of the store. "I don't see no one."

"Really? They were just there." She frowned. Had the tour wrapped up and they all left?

Frank shrugged again and said, "Sorry. Can't help you. That'll be forty-two-twenty-six."

And with that she had no answers to the cemetery mystery *and* an additional forty-two dollars and change added to her credit card balance. But at least she had wine glasses. Maybe she'd liberate a bottle from her stock and try to forget the mystery, the charge and her recent electrocution. Not to mention her encounter with rude doc.

She certainly had plenty to forget today.

Chapter Eight

"Jules."

"Yes, Natalie." There was a distinct tone of forced patience mingled with amusement in the eighteen-year old's voice as it came through the cell phone. Her unspoken words clearly said, *why are you calling instead of texting?*

Faced with the group of women in front of her now, Natalie felt justified in committing the cardinal sin—or at least *faux pas*—in her Gen Z employee's eyes.

Forcing a smile for the ladies' benefit, she said, "There are some...lovely ladies here at the register that say they spoke with you about meeting here tonight. But we have the book club in the meeting room already."

"Oh, right. Didn't I tell you? Maybe I mentioned it

to Harper instead. They have to meet tonight because of the full moon."

Not understanding the significance of that and thinking she was screwed and about to have nine very unhappy women on her hands, Natalie held up one finger to indicate she'd only be a moment, then turned to face away from them as she said, "Okay. But where did you plan on putting them if the meeting room is occupied?"

Through the open door to the meeting room, a bout of laughter rose above the loud din of conversation already coming from the book club members. It reinforced the fact they already had a full house tonight.

"That's the beauty of it. They don't want to be inside. They need to be outside," Jules explained.

"Outside. Okay. Like in the yard?"

She hoped they were looking to truly embrace nature since she hadn't dealt with the overgrown grass that desperately needed to be mowed. She also hoped they didn't sue her if they all came down with Lyme Disease from any ticks residing on her property.

"Actually, I suggested they meet on the roof."

"The roof?" She hadn't even been up there yet. "Is that safe? Will it hold them all?" she asked in a whisper.

"Yes and yes. I went up there and walked around. It's

solid and flat with a lip around the edge. The stairs have a railing. It seems safe enough."

"But why the roof and not the side yard?" she asked. Besides the fact there wasn't anywhere to sit. Getting exterior tables and chairs or at least a couple of garden benches was already on her ever-growing list.

"Because they're going sky clad."

Natalie's eyes widened at Jules's words. "Does that mean what I think it means?"

If memory served she'd seen that term before in a book she'd read and she was pretty sure it was what Wiccans, or maybe it was Druids, called dancing naked in the moonlight.

Jules laughed. "If you think it means *butt-ass naked*, then yes."

Natalie pivoted back to take in the group of ladies. Old. Young. Fat. Skinny. It was quite a mix of females. She pictured them all naked, dancing around her side yard. Then she pictured the old ladies—and old men— in town seeing them dancing naked in her yard.

"Okay. Good call. You're sure they're okay with being on the roof?"

"Oh, yeah. They're excited. They know the way upstairs. If you're busy, just send them up. I showed the group leader when she came in while you were in the hospital. Ooo, one more thing. One of the ladies makes tarot cards and asked if we could sell them in the store on consignment. Fifty-fifty split. Twenty dollars retail. They're gorgeous so I said yes. I tagged and put ten packs out in the spirituality section."

It seemed a lot happened while she'd been in the hospital. More than had happened in the month since she'd opened. And she hadn't even been a patient for a full twenty-four hours.

Biting her lip to keep from expressing the dozen or so concerns and questions she had, she let out a breath. "Okay. Thank you. Sorry to bother you at home."

"No problem. Text me if you have more questions!" Jules offered.

Text. Not call. Message received.

"Thanks." Natalie disconnected, put the cell down and turned to the tall woman with butt-length salt-and-pepper waves who was standing slightly in front of the others filling her shop. Ignoring the potential insurance ramifications, not to mention possible fire code violations, she said, "All right. If you don't need anything from me, you can go on up to the roof."

With a nod and a, "Blessed be," the group—or was it coven—ascended the stairs with an ethereal swish of long skirts and capes that looked enough like a scene out of Salem that Natalie had to shake off a chill.

Another bout of laughter drew her attention back to

her other guests. The Raunchy Romance Readers Book Club.

She moved to the open door and peeked inside. It seemed the iced tea and cookies had been a hit. She saw a cup in every hand and that the cookie platter was much emptier than it had been when they'd carried it inside. She could use a bit of a pick-me-up herself since she was going on ten hours in the shop.

Sneaking in to not disturb them, she grabbed a cup and poured a good amount of tea.

It was cold and thirst quenching, sweetened with just enough honey. It went down too smoothly and since there was still plenty left for the club members, Natalie poured herself a second cup, guiltily grabbed a cookie from the platter then crept back through the door to the shop.

Twenty-minutes later, the book club showed no signs up breaking up soon. Natalie had restocked the wine shelves, unpacked the latest book delivery, and replied to a question on the shop's Facebook page.

She was tired but somehow energized at the same time. As if her mind was sharp while her body settled into a state of warm, fuzzy relaxation. Like how she felt after a massage—back in the days when she could treat herself to such luxuries.

Maybe her coffee addiction was what kept her on

edge and feeling like she was spinning out of control all day. She needed to indulge in tea more often. It seemed even better than wine to raise her spirits and calm the anxiety but without dulling her mental abilities.

Liking the idea of becoming a tea drinker, she settled into the one cushy chair she had room for in the corner of the bookshop, whipped out her cell phone and started to shop for fun tea on Amazon. That led her to pretty teacups. Then intricately designed teaspoons. And a beehive shaped glass honey server...

She felt energized and inspired, even after the triple R ladies finally left and after the roof group came down —fully dressed again, thank goodness—an hour later.

Alone but not at all sleepy, Natalie decided now was the perfect time to make one of her book dreams come true.

Rainbow bookshelves.

What better time to rearrange the shelves than while there were no customers. No ringing phone. No deliveries pulling her away.

By morning when the store opened she'd have the front bookcase arranged by color, like a rainbow of books on the shelves. Just like she'd seen on TikTok, which she was now addicted to thanks to Jules showing her how to search #booktok on the app.

Inspired, she'd already unloaded all the books onto

the floor and was just starting to make a plan for reshelving them by color when a hard loud knock on the door made her jump.

After a yelp of surprise, she spun toward the door and scowled when she saw who it was.

Struggling to her feet from her spot on the floor, she stumbled to the door, flipped the lock and yanked it open.

"What are you doing here? Was my book club too loud for you?" she asked with as much attitude as she could muster in her Zen state.

"No. But I'd appreciate if they didn't trespass."

"What are you talking about?"

He folded his arms and didn't shrink at all in the face of her bad attitude. "I found two of your book club ladies peeping through my windows while the third one sat in the car like a getaway driver."

"I don't know what you're talking about."

"You don't believe me?"

Feeling feisty, she said, "Maybe I don't. Can your employees corroborate your story?"

"What employees?"

"I saw an older guy going in and out all day today."

As he frowned, she elaborated. "Grey hair. Walked with a limp."

"There was no one there but me today."

"Well then you've got a peeping tom but it wasn't my book club ladies."

"Fine. Believe what you want but the security cameras are getting installed tomorrow. Might want to tell your ladies that."

"I will *not,* thank you."

He rolled his eyes, then frowned at the row of red books she'd managed to reshelve before his interruption, his gaze moving down to the piles of books stacked on the floor she had yet to organize. "What are you doing?"

"Organizing the books by color. Like a rainbow."

He shook his head and after a distinctly judgmental glance, turned and with a tinkling of the bell and a rudely loud slam of the door, he was gone.

Eyes narrowed in anger—part for his interrupting her and part over the accusation—she watched him stride away as she locked the door.

And as the same old man she'd mentioned and he'd denied knowing followed him back to the warehouse she let out a loud snort.

"Rude *and* a liar."

She turned back to her project. At least men in books made her happy. Book boyfriends were the only men worth giving her time to.

Chapter Nine

Opening time seemed to come earlier than usual since Natalie didn't get to bed, and then not to sleep, until the wee hours of the morning.

She was tired but she still felt good. Unshowered and with only half a cup of coffee in her system, she still unlocked the door with a smile and a greeting for the old lady walking past.

All that earned her was a frown and a stare from the woman, who bustled off a little faster, all while glancing over her shoulder suspiciously at Natalie.

Even that couldn't bring her mood down today. Especially when she looked at her beautiful new book display. She was just admiring it when the door flung open and Jules barreled in.

Natalie frowned. "Aren't you supposed to be in school?"

"It's finals week. This is more important anyway."

"More important than finals?"

"I had one this morning. I don't have another one until later today. But listen—Nice rainbow shelves by the way." Jules eyeballed the new display that had kept Natalie up way past her bedtime before turning back.

"Thanks, and I'm listening."

The door opened again and Harper blew in like a hurricane. "WBNG wants to interview you!"

Jules scowled. "Way to steal my thunder."

"Sorry, Jules. I just saw the message and couldn't wait."

"What message? And how do you both know about this and not me?"

"They private messaged the shop's Instagram," Julia began.

"We both have the log in so we can post," Harper added.

And Natalie didn't remember to check for messages on Instagram on a good day. Never mind on a day after she'd barely slept. In the interest of saving her sanity she'd turned off all notifications on her phone. She definitely hadn't checked this morning after rolling out of bed barely half an hour before opening.

"What do they want to interview me about?" She was starting to get excited. If they did a feature about the shop it could bring in a ton of new business—

"About your getting electrocuted," Harper revealed.

Natalie's shoulders fell along with her excitement. She shook her head. "I don't know—"

"You have to do it. Think of the publicity," Jules cried.

"I agree with Jules." Harper nodded. "This could be big for the shop."

Natalie drew in a breath and let it out. "Fine. When?"

Later that afternoon, after making a fool of herself on WBNG and with the spirit of a dead guy relentlessly following her around the shop, she truly regretted that earlier decision to do the interview.

"Are you sure you're okay?" Jules asked.

"Yes, I'm fine."

Jules narrowed her eyes at her. "Are you sure? You told me you could see dead people."

"I know. I think it's just my vision is off. Between the lights and the sun glare and the electrocution and all, my eyes are a little messed up. I couldn't see clearly. People looked, you know, ghostly," she lied, pretty smoothly she thought. "Thanks for not telling Harper what I told you, by the way. It's so embarrassing."

"Sure. No problem."

Mere seconds after spewing she could see dead people to Jules, Natalie had decided she couldn't tell anyone about this.

If it were true, they'd think she was crazy. If it weren't true, they'd force her to go to the hospital again. She couldn't afford that bill or to have the shop closed. She felt fine physically. Really the only symptom was Gabe the talking ghost and his creepy friends who didn't respect her personal space.

At least only Gabe was inside the shop with her now. Well, Gabe and Jules who was still looking at her like she'd lost it.

"I'm fine. I promise. I'll call you—I mean *text* you if I start to feel funny."

"Or Harper if I don't answer. I'll be in my final for a couple of hours. But Harper said she was going back to the house to do some work."

And thank God she hadn't told Harper about the dead people after the interview. She wouldn't be as easy to lie to as Jules. More than that, she'd probably want to use the idea in a book and need to interview her for ghost details or something.

Turning Jules toward the door, she said, "I promise to call Harper too. Now go. Do great on your final. Get an A. Graduate and come work more hours for me before you leave me to start college this fall."

With her hand on the knob, Jules finally nodded. "Okay. I'll check on you as soon as I'm done with the test."

"Good. I'll await your text. Good luck."

When the door finally closed behind the girl Natalie crumbled back against the front display table. And there was Gabe, right in front of her. Much too close, as usual.

Dead people really had no sense of personal space.

"Will you give me some room, please?" she hissed out of the side of her mouth so no one in the shop would hear her talking to what appeared to be no one.

Hell, she might be speaking to no one for all she knew. She still wasn't convinced Gabe wasn't caused by some brain bleed.

"Why aren't you looking for who killed me?" he demanded.

He followed her as she made her way to the register counter. "Because I have a shop to run and bills to pay. I'll work on your case later. After I close."

"There's treasure," he said in a sing-song tone.

She let out a snort of a laugh loud enough to draw

the attention of the woman perusing the Women's Fiction section.

"Sorry." Natalie cringed and pointed to the cell phone in her hand as an excuse for her outburst. "Funny cat video."

As the woman raised her brows then returned to some book with a pastel beach cover that pretty much looked like all the books on the shelf next to it, Gabe put his ghostly finger right in Natalie's face.

"What's wrong with you? That treasure would pay off all your bills. Plus set you up for the rest of your life. What are you? Like forty years old? Forty-five?"

"What? No. I'm not even forty yet, thank you," she whispered with a scowl. She was holding on to the final months of being thirty-nine with both hands and no ghost was going to take that from her.

Forty-five. Hmph.

Since Gabe insisted on having this conversation in front of customers, while insulting her, she pushed an earbud into her ear so it would look like she was speaking on the phone.

"Wouldn't you like to be retired at under forty?" he asked. "And, upside, you get one hundred percent of the treasure since your partner—me—is dead."

"You saying the word *treasure* over and over again is not making me have any more faith in you, you know. In fact, it's making me believe your story even less."

His blue eyes widened. "My *story*? What do you mean? I was murdered. Did you not see the knife in my back?" He twisted for her to see the disturbing evidence yet again.

"I saw. But how do I know how that happened? You said yourself you don't even know who stabbed you," she whispered. Even if the customer did believe she was speaking on the cell phone, talking about stabbings probably wouldn't be viewed as an appropriate topic of conversation.

"I couldn't see them because—obviously—they were behind me. Duh." He spread his hands wide. "Besides, I asked around. Apparently we don't remember the exact moment of our death."

"Asked around as in you asked the *other ghosts*?" she hissed after a glance around her.

"Yeah." He nodded.

"So how do you know it wasn't just a normal everyday mugging gone wrong?" she asked.

"Because I was only steps away from discovering the treasure."

"Pirate treasure?" she asked with amusement. "Was it buried? Is there a map with a big X marking the spot? Or no. Wait. Nazi treasure. Is it the holy grail? Is that why you're dressed like Indiana Jones? And about that...are you stuck in the clothes you died in forever? Can you take them off?"

He ignored her questions and narrowed his eyes at her with a glare. "It's the largest, most valuable cache of Prohibition-era wealth in history. Hidden by a gangster before he was killed. And I wasn't the only one looking for it. Hence the knife in the back."

She let out a sigh and after another glance at the woman shopping said, "Did it happen here in town? Is that why you're stuck *haunting here?*" she whispered.

"No. I'm not stuck in the place where I died. I'm tethered to my body."

She nodded. "So your body is here in Mudville?"

"Is that where we are?" He glanced out the door. "Where the hell is Mudville? What state?"

"Upstate New York. Near Binghamton."

He nodded.

"So you were buried here..."

"Oh, I'm not buried." He let out a snort.

"What do you mean?" she frowned.

Was he cremated? And if so were his ashes in a jar on someone's mantle? Someone she was going to have to go tell their loved one had been murdered. Yeah, that was going to go over well.

"My body's over there." He pointed to the warehouse.

Natalie's eyes popped wide as pieces of the puzzle flew together in her mind.

Mary Brimley claiming she saw a body being carried in by two men out of the back of a pick-up truck. Hot doctor storming over here upset about a peeping tom. The rumors he was a serial killer or an assassin. And now a ghost claiming he was murdered and his body was inside.

Oh. My. God.

Chapter Ten

"You okay? You look kinda pale." Ghost Gabe leaned closer to peer into Natalie's face.

She barely got enough breath into her lungs to say, "Your body... is in the warehouse?"

He nodded. "Yup. Cut up in pieces."

The room swayed and so did Natalie. She grabbed for the edge of the counter, bracing herself as she repeated, "Pieces?"

She pressed one hand to the base of her throat as she felt the vomit threatening to rise. She'd asked the murderer out for drinks. She could have been his next victim. Trapped in the warehouse for eternity with Gabe. In pieces!

"Maybe you should sit down." Gabe reached for the stool behind the counter, which his ghost hand passed right through. "Shit. I keep forgetting I'm not corporeal anymore."

"*Corporeal*. Good word, my brother." A man with what looked like two gunshot wounds to the chest hooked a thumb toward Natalie. "I assume she can still see us since she looks like she's going to pass out."

"Oh, God. Please. Not more of you," she begged on a breath.

"Maybe you should keep the others outside and give her some space?" Gabe suggested.

Others. She remembered the crowd at the interview. If they all came inside... She couldn't even face the thought of it.

That was it. It was settled. She'd have to sell. Move. Hide. Possibly in a hospital. In the psych ward. But there were probably ghosts in the hospital too. Lots of them...

With one more glance at her, the newcomer said, "Sure. We'll be in the graveyard if you want to join later. That chick who moved into the house next door doesn't close her curtains."

The ghost, dressed in a bowling shirt, waggled his eyebrows then walked through the door. As in *through* the door.

"Is he..." She swallowed and tried again. "Is his body in the warehouse too?"

"Oh, no. He's actually buried in the graveyard. Got

shot in the parking lot of a bar after a card game back in the eighties."

She blew out a breath. Okay. She could deal with this.

Step one, call the authorities. She wouldn't have to tell the sheriff she could see ghosts. Just that he needed to search the warehouse because she'd noticed something suspicious.

Then they would find the body... Body or *bodies*, plural.

She raised her gaze to Gabe. "Are there more? More than you. Over there?"

"More bodies?" he asked.

She nodded.

"Oh, yeah. There are a few of us."

She flattened her palms against the counter then leaned her forehead on the cool wooden surface in an attempt to remain on her feet and not vomit.

"I think she wants to check out. I'd help you but..." Gabe's voice brought her head back up and there stood the woman with her book selection in one hand and a distinctly judgmental expression on her pinched face.

This was insane. Besides talking to a murdered ghost and finding out her neighbor was both a killer and a dismember-er, she was running on only a few hours' sleep and no food. And through it all, she had to run this shop.

But the customers came first. Natalie forced a smile. "Ready?"

"I've been ready." The old lady scowled.

Her smile wavered but held. "Of course."

With shaking hands she dispatched with the woman as fast as possible, but she did *not* give her a free Once Upon a Vine bookmark like she always did with a book purchase. Rudeness had consequences.

When she and Gabe were finally alone again—and while she considered how her relief about being alone with a ghost had to be proof of brain damage or psychosis—Natalie reached for her phone.

"What are you doing?" he asked.

"Calling the sheriff about your body."

"Thank you!" He flung his arms up in the air. "It's about damn time."

Looking satisfied, Gabe folded his arms, leaned back against a bookcase, and promptly fell backwards all the way through it.

Shaking her head at him and the string of cuss words she could hear coming from the other side of the shelving unit, she pressed the phone to her ear and waited.

"Mudville Sheriff's Department."

"Um, hi. I'd like to report a..." A what?

Murder? No. She couldn't explain that. How would she know that there had been a murder if she hadn't talked to Gabe?

"Report a what?" the man on the other end of the call asked. "Ma'am?"

Bracing herself, she said, "I'd like to report a dead body."

———

She had to give credit to the Mudville Sheriff's Department. One very handsome and prompt Deputy Carson Bekker arrived in less than ten minutes.

Ten minutes during which she'd paced and gnawed on her fingernails while Gabe watched and told her to relax.

The deputy, alluring in his small-town khaki uniform, had the required tiny notebook like she'd seen on plenty of shows but never in real life. The pen and pad were out, ready for her statement.

They'd already covered who she was and how long she'd been the owner of the shop. Now came the touchy part. He raised his gaze to her and said, "You said something about a dead body?"

"Yes. It's in the warehouse next door."

"And you know this how?"

"I, uh, saw it being carried in."

"You saw the actual body being carried in?" he asked.

"Yes."

"When?"

Shit. She shot a sideways look at Gabe who answered, "Last week."

"Last week," she repeated.

"Do you remember which day?"

Gabe shook his head.

"No. I'm so sorry. I don't. I've been so busy with the shop, all the days blend together." She delivered that with a self-deprecating smile.

"That's good. Flirt with him. That'll throw him off." Gabe nodded.

Natalie frowned, hoping it told him she didn't need his commentary distracting her. She was nervous enough.

"And did you see an actual body?" the deputy asked.

She glanced at Gabe who said, "I was wrapped in plastic."

"It was um, wrapped in plastic," she repeated.

The deputy lowered the pad and pen. "So you saw something in plastic. Not a body."

Shit-shit-shit. She should have thought this through better.

She scrambled to salvage the situation. "It was body sized."

He flipped the notebook closed. In her mind he might as well have said *case closed*.

"I saw the body too," she lied.

He raised sandy-colored brows. "You did?"

"Yes. I didn't want to tell you because, well, I was peeking in the warehouse windows after I saw the body being carried in. I didn't tell you right away because I was afraid that was a crime."

He tipped his head. "It is trespassing but given the circumstances...you're not the first to report suspicious items being brought into the warehouse."

Thank goodness for the nosy old folks of Mudville corroborating her story. Or Gabe's story, really.

The deputy drew in a chest expanding breath then nodded. "All right. I'll go over and check it out."

"Thank you!" she and Gabe said at the same time. Her with gratitude. Gabe with attitude.

The deputy pulled open the door and stepped through. When he paused to turn back to her she almost crashed into him and Gabe passed through her.

With a shiver, she took a step back and said, "Sorry."

He reached into the breast pocket of his uniform. "Here's my card. If you remember anything else, call me."

"Okay."

With a nod he started walking toward the warehouse.

"Go on. Follow him," Gabe said much too close to her ear.

She could almost feel his ghostly breath on her skin. With another shiver she took a step back from the dead guy who thought it was all right to be attached to her at the hip.

"You think I should?" she whispered.

"Yes! What if the doctor lies? I can be there to tell you. And you can tell the deputy."

This was a risky, her knowing things she had no viable way of knowing. But Gabe was right. They couldn't trust the hot murdering doc.

"All right." She took off at a trot, Gabe at her side.

She covered the distance in time to hear the deputy say, "There's been a report of a dead body here on the premises."

"Of course there was." Hot doc's eyes zeroed in on Natalie where she'd stopped a couple of yards behind the deputy.

He folded his arms and stood his ground.

"He didn't deny it," she said mostly to Gabe although the deputy glanced over his shoulder at her before focusing back on the doctor.

"Sir. Is there a body in this building?" Deputy Bekker asked.

"Of course there's a body in this building. More than one. It's a cadaver lab." He pointed to the logo embroidered on the chest of his shirt. It read *The Human Institute*. "We're a research facility."

Natalie spun to face Gabe.

"Why didn't you say that?" she mouthed.

He shrugged in response.

Meanwhile, after a chuckle from Bekker and a few exchanged words, it looked like the deputy and hot doc were getting buddy-buddy. Apparently, Deputy Bekker was going to get a tour of the warehouse.

And when Natalie went to follow, hot doc shot her a glare and then unceremoniously slammed the door right in her face.

Fine. So he wasn't a deranged serial killer but he was still the rudest man she'd ever met.

She spun on her heel to leave when Gabe blocked her path. "Where are you going?"

"I'm leaving."

"You can't leave. Even if he didn't kill me, he has my body. He could have answers."

"What kind of answers?"

"Where my body was found. What the police report said. Clues about the knife wound, like was the assailant right-handed or left-handed. Short or tall. Male or female."

"You really think he could help?" she asked.

"Do you have any other leads?" Gabe countered.

"No. Okay. Fine. I'll talk to him. But you saw how rude he was to me."

"Yes. Very rude." Gabe rolled his eyes. "You'll get over it. I won't get over this." He turned his deadly knife wound toward her. And of course, she felt bad enough to give in.

"One day this guilt ploy of yours is going to stop working on me," she warned and moved to lean on the building next to the door.

"No, it won't." Gabe smiled. He folded his arms and leaned next to her...and fell through the wall.

Chapter Eleven

It was a long five minutes later when Gabe burst through the door, startling her. "Deputy's on his way out."

"What did they do in there for so long?" she asked.

"Talked mostly. Apparently they're both former military. Then they had a good old look at my brain, which the doctor had conveniently sawed in half."

She pressed a hand to her churning stomach. "Okay. We can't talk about stuff like that or I'll puke."

"Wimp," he mumbled as the door opened.

The deputy stopped in the doorway when he saw her. "Miss Chase. Was there something else?"

"No. I just wanted to talk to the doctor. To apologize," she added, thinking that sounded legitimate.

The deputy nodded to her and the doctor and then strode off to where his official vehicle was still parked at her shop.

That left Natalie with a very unhappy looking hot doctor, but not for long she feared.

With one hand on the door and a stony expression on his unfairly attractive features, he said, "I don't want your apology. I want you to leave me alone."

He moved to slam the door but she was faster. She shoved her foot in the doorway and braced one palm on the door to hold it open.

Talking fast because he was definitely stronger than her, she said, "Look. I know you hate me but I had a very good reason for what I did."

"Oh, yeah?" His laugh sounded bitter. "What's that?"

She couldn't see any way around it except to tell him. "Ever since I... died I've been seeing things."

"Delusions."

"No. Ghosts." She dared to raise her gaze to his after that confession.

Dark brows shot up over ocean-colored eyes. "Ghosts."

"Yes. One of them is one of your cadavers."

"One of mine. And you know this how?"

"He told me."

"He told you."

"Are you going to just keep repeating what I say?" She scowled.

"Look. I know what happens to a body when it's hit with the kind of voltage you were—"

"I'm not crazy!" She stomped her foot to reinforce the point.

"I'm not saying you are. I'm saying the physical results of a shock like that affect the brain—"

"Yeah. I bet he's dying to cut your brain in half and see for himself. I've seen the saw. He could do it." Gabe's comment reminded her of his presence.

"I can prove it to you. His name is Gabe—"

"Miller," Gabe interrupted.

"What?" She turned to face him.

"Gabriel Allen Miller. That's my full name," Gabe supplied.

She pivoted back. "His name is Gabriel Allen Miller and he's dressed like Indiana Jones—"

"No. I'm naked," Gabe corrected.

"Naked?" she asked, facing him again.

"Yes. Of course. You think he left me dressed to cut me into pieces. You think half my head is sitting on a shelf wearing my hat? Jesus, woman. Think a little bit." Gabe shook his head.

"Sorry. Jeez. You're my first cadaver. What do I know?" She turned back to hot doc and saw him watching her with brows high.

"Uh, who are you talking to?" he asked.

"Gabe. Your cadaver."

"I don't have a cadaver named Gabe," he said with more patience than he'd ever shown with her since she'd first met him. The kind of patience people used with a deranged person they were afraid of setting off.

"Yes, you do. He says his body is inside here and in pieces. Do you have a male body? One that you cut the brain in half. Oh! Wait. I almost forgot. He was killed by a knife in the back." She leaned back to glance behind Gabe. "A knife with what looks like a bone handle— That's nice. Is that an antique?"

Gabe twisted to try to see the knife in his back. "Don't know. I never saw it."

"Didn't you ever look in a mirror? Wait, can you see your reflection or is it a vampire kind of situation?"

He shrugged. "Don't know. I never tried."

"You should. I have a mirror. We'll look later at the shop. Remind me." She glanced back to hot doc. "So, do you have a male cadaver who died of a stab wound whose head you sawed in half or not?"

There was the briefest of pauses before he nodded slowly. "I do. But he was listed as a John Doe."

She spun back to Gabe. "You died as a John Doe? Why didn't you tell me that?"

"I'm sorry. I didn't know." He shrugged.

She turned back and saw hot doc looking about ready to flee. Or maybe to call Deputy Bekker back and have him lock her up.

Turning back to Gabe she said, "What else have you got that will convince him I'm not crazy?"

"Um. There are two other cadavers in there with me. One is an old lady with short gray hair. Smoker. Lung cancer. Named Ethel."

She repeated that information to hot doc. When his eyes widened she knew she'd hit a nerve.

"Walk through him," she said to Gabe.

"What? Why?"

"Because I want him to know you're really here. Really a ghost. Otherwise he's going to think I broke in and read his files or something."

"Fine." Looking unhappy, Gabe walked through the hot doc.

He frowned as he gave a visible shudder. "What...the fuck?"

"That was Gabe." She glanced to Gabe. "At least now that I know you're a John Doe, we can contact the police who were on your case and give them your identity. Maybe they can find your killer and you can stop haunting me."

"I'm not haunting you. I'm asking for a favor. You want to see haunting? I'll bring over that Revolutionary War ghost in the cemetery who had his limbs rot off from gangrene before he died. *That's* haunting."

She wrinkled her nose. "Please don't."

Realizing hot doc had gone suspiciously quiet she focused on him. "You all right, doc?"

He was still hot as hell, but he'd gone pale beneath his tan.

"Tell me about the third cadaver inside," he said, testing her.

She turned her gaze to Gabe as he said, "Myra. Ninety-nine years old. Died in her sleep. Put in her will she wanted her body donated to science. Nice lady."

"Myra. Ninety-nine. Died in her sleep," Natalie repeated.

Hot doc braced his palm high on the doorframe and leaned heavily against it.

"I think we need to talk." He glanced around them as if looking for Gabe. "All three of us."

"Sure. You, uh, wanna do this inside my place? There are less ghosts."

His nostrils flared as he drew in a deep breath. "How many ghosts are here?"

"Um." She glanced around her. "There's a guy

hanging around the train tracks. Missing half his jaw. He's pretty haunting," she said to Gabe.

He nodded. "Yeah. I forgot about him. He's up there on the haunting scale."

Natalie continued, "There's your two ladies here, of course. They keep poking their heads through the door then disappearing. Actually, there are less hanging around than usual. Like that old guy who follows you around isn't here. It must be that ghost party in the cemetery gunshot wound guy told you about."

She said that last part to Gabe.

Hot doc's eyes got wider. He swallowed. "And how many ghosts do you have in your shop?"

"Just Gabe for now. He told them all they're not allowed inside. Thank you for that by the way."

Gabe nodded. "You're most welcome."

"Let's go." Hot doc pushed off the doorframe, then halted. "You have any booze at your place?"

She raised a brow. "It's a wine shop so...yeah."

"*Real* booze," he corrected.

Narrowing her gaze at him she finally nodded. "Yes. I have real booze."

"Good. Let's go." He took a step then said, "Is he coming?"

"He's already halfway there. Wait, he stopped to talk

to train track dude. Okay, they're done now. He's inside."

Hot doc shot her a sideways glance.

"Stop looking at me like I'm crazy."

He drew in a breath then let it out. "That's the problem. If you're crazy, then so am I, because I believe you."

Chapter Twelve

The doctor's dark brows drew low as he stared at the wine glass filled with yellow liquid she'd set in front of him.

"Don't worry. It's not wine."

He pulled his mouth to the side and picked up the glass that looked tiny in his large hands. He knocked back the contents then coughed. Frowning deeper he said, "Christ. What the hell was that?"

"Limoncello. My friend Harper brought me a bottle as a welcome. She and her aunt make it. Isn't that amazing?"

"Yeah. Great." He set the glass down and leaned back against the sofa cushion.

Natalie sat in the upholstered chair opposite. It seemed she'd found another use for the meeting space. It functioned nicely as a living room for when she entertained.

Maybe she'd host a party.

She imagined decorating the space, which of course turned her mind to Christmas. Unlike her old apartment in the city, she'd be able to have a huge tree in here. Ooo, maybe she'd decorate it with bookish ornaments...

Hot doc had been silent for so long she put her mental Christmas planning on hold and turned her attention to him. Even with him looking kind of in shock and still scowling from the limoncello, he easily remained one of the best-looking men she'd ever met.

"Stop drooling over him and ask him some questions," Gabe prodded.

Annoyed at the disturbance in her admiring the man she was entertaining, Natalie asked, "You okay there, doc?"

"Liam."

"Excuse me?"

"My name. It's Liam."

She frowned. "That's not what I heard."

His brows rose. "I don't know what you heard, but that's my name."

She pawed her memory for everything Bethany and Harper had said. She was sure she would have remembered if they'd said a romance novel worthy name like Liam.

"It's short for William," he continued.

"Ah. Yeah. That's right. Doctor William Walsh. Okay. So, are you okay, Liam?" she asked again.

"That wasn't the question I was thinking of you asking him. How about where'd you get the body, Liam? How many more pieces are you going to hack it into, Liam? What the hell are you looking for inside Gabe's brain anyway, Liam?" Gabe listed his snarky questions with a scowl.

She ignored the nagging ghost and worked to focus on lusting over Liam, who was much less rude now that he was in shock about his cadavers being able to talk.

Sawing them into pieces was going to be ruined for him now, although she couldn't say she was disappointed by that. Maybe he'd stop that part. The whole process sounded barbaric.

"I'll be fine as long as I don't have any more of that stuff." He eyed the bottle of yellow liquid on the table. "So you only started seeing them after you were electrocuted?"

She nodded.

"What would have caused that?" Since he seemed to be talking more to himself than to her and since she didn't have an answer either way she remained quiet as he continued, "Maybe the electricity activated a part of your brain that's normally inactive for most people. And if that's true, then perhaps some of those psychics who claim a connection to the deceased aren't faking, but also have the same brain center activated."

"Told you. His jonesing to saw into that pretty little head of yours."

She twisted to look at Gabe. "Aw, you think I'm pretty?"

Gabe rolled his eyes. "Not the point."

"Well, thank you anyway."

"You're welcome," Gabe answered flatly.

She glanced back and saw Liam staring at her.

"You really are talking to him," he said.

"I am. He thinks you're dying to get a look at my brain. To see what the shock did."

Liam bobbed his head to one side. "He's not wrong."

Gabe let out a *hmph* while Natalie was back to wondering if a man who enjoyed cutting up bodies so much was really a good choice for her first Mudville crush.

"Are there any more symptoms?" he asked, leaning forward and pinning her with that emerald gaze.

"Not really. I was pretty wired last night after the

book club meeting, when usually I'm exhausted at the end of the day."

"Did you have coffee late in the day?" Now he was starting to sound like an actual doctor.

She flashed back to the little old doctor she'd gotten her vaccines from back in the city. That made it feel extra icky that she'd been imagining Liam shirtless because she definitely hadn't wanted to see her old doctor shirtless.

He was looking at her expectantly. Why? Oh, right. He'd asked about coffee. "I only had some iced tea during the meeting."

"That's got caffeine."

"Fine. That's not a symptom. So no. No other ill effects from being electrocuted and dying except now every ghost in Mudville can talk to me. I think that's symptoms enough. Don't you?"

"I'm just trying to figure this out." He was so calm and logical. Cold, almost.

She might have liked it better when he'd been rude. She didn't like this new unfeeling analytical research-mode.

"How about figuring out *who killed me*!" Gabe interjected.

Right. Gabe.

"While you're working on why I can suddenly see ghosts, can I ask you a few questions about Gabe?"

When he looked at her with a blank expression, she added, "Your male cadaver. I promised I'd try and help figure out who murdered him."

His eyes shifted around the room again. "Is he, uh, still here?"

"Yes."

"Where?"

"Standing next to me."

"Tell him I'm sorry I cut his brain in half." Liam looked a little sick as he said it.

"He says he forgives you," she said.

Gabe's eyes flew wide. "I did not say that. Ooo. You are such a liar."

She resisted the urge to shush Gabe and concentrated on what information she needed from Liam. "You said he was a John Doe. Do you know where he was murdered?"

"He came through the anatomical donation program at Albany Medical College."

"So maybe you were killed somewhere near there," she directed to Gabe. "It makes sense that if the local police couldn't identify you they'd donate your body to the nearest... whatever he said."

"Body donor program," Liam supplied.

"That," she said tipping her head toward Liam. "Were you near Albany before you died?"

"Kind of. I was all over the Hudson Valley looking for the treasure. Ulster, Dutchess."

"There you go with the treasure again." She rolled her eyes.

"I'm not making it up. Dutch Schultz is supposed to have buried a box filled with gold and diamonds in that area. He was mostly in the Bronx but his illegal business dealings extended upstate. The largest moonshine producer in New York State was in Dutchess County. Dutch was murdered in 1935, I believe before retrieving the treasure."

She frowned. "I've heard of Dutch Schultz. Why didn't you lead with the fact this treasure belonged to a famous bootlegger?"

"Uh, what now?" Liam asked.

Natalie hooked a thumb toward Gabe. "He's been talking about buried treasure all day. I was picturing like a big pirate chest and Black Beard. But this seems a little more believable. Like it could be real."

"I spent the last ten years of my life looking for it. Of course it's real." Gabe scowled.

"Anyway, he was in that area looking for Dutch Schultz's gold and diamonds so it's possible that's where he was murdered. If I can give the police his name, it might help."

Liam had taken out his cell phone and typed

something as he asked, "And how are you going to do that? Tell them you know their murdered John Doe's name because his ghost told you?"

Liam had obviously recovered from the shock. He was getting snarky again.

"No. Maybe I could leave an anonymous tip. There are tip lines just for that sort of thing." Although she should probably try to find a pay phone to make the call so it couldn't be tracked to her.

Were there still pay phones? Maybe there was an online tip line. She could log in to the computer at the library...

"The police will probably think it's a mugging if they don't know that he was looking for a century old treasure. *That* detail seems like the biggest clue to whom might have killed him," Liam said.

"Yes! That's what I've been saying. I like him. You have my permission to keep seeing him."

She sent Gabe a glare then turned back to Liam. "He agrees with you that the treasure and the murder were connected. So should my anonymous tip include what Gabe knows about the treasure?"

Gabe covered his face with his hands in frustration. "No! Then the cops will just go find it and keep it for themselves. If whoever murdered me didn't find it already. *You* need to look for it. I'm telling you I was so close to finding it. That's why I was killed."

She was going to ignore Gabe until Liam said, "No. I don't think you should tell the police about the treasure. I think we should look for it ourselves. You and me. Together."

"Um, what?" That was from Gabe because Natalie was temporarily speechless.

Chapter Thirteen

"YES. YES. YES!"

Harper had squealed with such enthusiasm Natalie took a step backward, pinning herself against the front window.

"Jules?" Harper asked.

Julia shrugged. "Sure. I love it here and I didn't have any other plans for the summer."

"I might be gone for a few days. And with the book clubs, you'll have to stay open late a couple of nights. Are you sure you can handle the shop plus all the meetings that are scheduled?" Natalie asked.

A part of her wanted them to say no. That she couldn't go on this hair-brained treasure hunting excursion with hot doc Liam.

Harper waved away her concern. "No problem. And

if I get in the weeds, I can call Agnes or Stone to come help me."

"Now I feel bad. I didn't mean to rope your aunt and your fiancé into helping me out too. I can just put up a sign and close for a few day—"

"Stop. There's no reason to close. You have us. Besides, you deserve to have a life outside of this shop. And your mother will be disappointed if you don't come," Harper pointed out.

The stab of guilt over that lie cut right through her chest. But what could she do? Tell them she was taking two or three days off to look for the buried treasure Gabe the ghost had told her about?

"Yeah, I guess. But seriously. Thank you both so much."

"It's going to be fun. Can I play my own music?" Jules asked.

She considered Jules's age compared to that of the average customer and hid a cringe. "Um, yeah. Sure. Just not too loud, okay?"

"Not too loud. I promise. Can I bring Taco to work?"

"Taco?" Natalie smiled when realization hit. "Is that what you named the dog?"

Julia nodded. "It seemed to fit. You know?"

"One hundred percent. Yes, you can bring Taco to work."

"Jules, remember to post pics of him on the socials. Dogs and cats are social media gold," Harper reminded.

As if on cue, Mr. Darcy hopped up on the windowsill and stretched luxuriously beneath the sun streaming in.

"Of course." Jules nodded, whipping out her phone and lining up a shot of him.

It seemed the store was going to be in good hands, although the idea of being so easily replaced in her own shop was kind of hard to swallow.

The tinkling of the bell above the door had all of their heads turning, even Mr. Darcy's, as in walked Liam, followed closely by Gabe.

They represented the totality of the men currently in her life. One was dead. The other an ass. And they both only wanted her for her ability to help look for the treasure. How sad was that?

"How early can you be ready to go tomorrow?" Liam asked, right there in front of Harper and Jules.

And by their wide-eyed expressions they were as surprised by his bursting in as she was, but she was sure for different reasons.

"Um, Liam, this is Harper and Julia. And this is Liam. He runs The Human Institute in the warehouse next door. It's a research facility. And he's going downstate with me because he has an appointment in Albany. I drive right past there on the way to visit my *mother,* so we figured we'd carpool."

There, that was a pretty good excuse if she did say so herself.

But she still had to make sure Liam was onboard with it. She turned to face him and widened her eyes in a way she hoped communicated what lies she'd told. Lies she needed him to back up.

Gabe literally doubled over laughing. When he came up for a breath, he said, "Oh, man. You are the worst liar."

She sent him a glare then focused back on Liam.

He looked as if he was barely restraining himself from rolling his eyes at her.

Too bad. He wasn't the one who would be judged for saying he could talk to ghosts. She was.

"And I can be ready to leave as early as you need me to be," she continued in answer to his original question.

"Then I'll be over at zero-seven hundred. They open at ten." His gaze shot to Harper and Jules. "The, uh, place... in Albany...where I have my appointment." One brow cocked up as his eyes shifted to Natalie. "Good?"

"Good," she echoed wishing this conversation would end.

Meanwhile, Harper and Jules looked ready to burst, probably with a dozen or so unasked questions. She was going to be in for an inquisition when Liam left. She only hoped she was up for the challenge.

"Do you need a wake-up call?" he asked.

"No. I think I can manage to set my alarm." She scowled.

"All right. See you in the morning."

"Mm-hm."

As she'd predicted the door had barely closed behind him—but not Gabe who stayed to enjoy the show—when they pounced.

"Hottie doctor's name is Liam? That's crazy swoony." Jules clutched her heart.

Harper's brows rose high. "So, you and hot doc are buddies and you didn't tell me. Which says to me that there's something more going on between you than just friendship. You two are going away together?"

Natalie shook her head. "There's nothing romantic. And there won't be. I promise you. I'm giving him a ride because I owe him… because I called the sheriff on him yesterday."

"Lies. Lies. Lies." Gabe shook his head while looking amused.

Annoyed with the heckling from her audience, she swiped at Gabe with one hand, hoping he'd go away.

When Harper frowned at the random motion Natalie said, "Bug."

Jules's eyes popped wide. "You called the sheriff on him?"

"I thought I saw a body being carried inside so I called the sheriff's department and asked them to search the warehouse. Which of course pissed off hot doc because there are bodies inside. Because it's a cadaver lab. Apparently he studies human bodies."

"Holy cow. He works with dead people, for real?" Jules pressed her palms to her cheeks.

"Cadaver lab." Harper's eyes took on a faraway quality before she turned her gaze to Jules and Natalie. "Am I crazy or does this have all the makings for a great romance novel? A female book shop owner. The hot doctor next door. She thinks he's a serial killer... because of the bodies. But he's really doing important research in his cadaver lab."

"That's not a romance novel. It's my life and no, you cannot write a book about it," Natalie insisted.

Jules shook her head. "Yeah, she's just gonna do it anyway."

Harper narrowed her eyes at Jules before turning back to Natalie. "Just think about it. While on your road trip with hot doc Liam." She broke out into a smile, which Jules mirrored.

It seemed this was the perfect time to get out of town for a few days. Maybe by the time she got back they'd have gotten over this juvenile notion of her and Liam.

"They're never going to let up on you about him." Next to her Gabe folded his arms and leaned back against the windowsill... and fell onto the sidewalk outside.

Good. It was what he deserved for speaking what she knew was the truth, even if she didn't want to hear it.

Chapter Fourteen

"You're ready." Liam made the statement with an insulting amount of surprise in his tone.

Mouth screwed up unhappily, she said, "I told you I would be."

In fact, she'd set her alarm for dawn so she wouldn't be late.

"I thought I'd drive." Her gaze moved over the expanse of the big black Jeep parked right in front of her shop blocking the front window display. Of course it was his.

Her car would definitely use less gas. And if they were going to split travel expenses equally, his gas guzzler was going to break her budget.

He drew back. "I'd rather drive how ever many hours

it takes us to get there than have to endure sitting in the passenger seat with *you* driving."

Could the man be any ruder? Jeez. "How many miles a gallon that thing get? A whole eight?"

"What do you care? I'm paying for my own gas."

"Fine."

Letting him come was a bad idea. Even if the last person who'd gone looking for this treasure had ended up dead, and even though Liam's bulk could provide protection as well as a bigger, better target for the killer, she wasn't sure it was worth having him tag along.

She grabbed her bag off the floor then glanced back at Mr. Darcy, asleep above the non-fiction section.

He'd somehow found his way inside on his own again last night even though he'd followed Harper outside when she'd left yesterday. Natalie supposed he would keep finding his way in and out while she was gone, but just in case, she'd left him food and water and an emergency litter box, which she'd seen him using yesterday right before she saw him running around outside not five minutes later.

Annoying cat. And of course, he was a male. Maybe that was a trait among all males. She eyed Liam as she locked the shop door and stashed the key beneath the flowerpot as agreed upon with Harper and Jules.

"Oh, that's real secure," he commented.

"I forgot to get another key cut yesterday."

"Hmph." Even his grunt sounded judgmental.

She ignored it and stood next to the Jeep's passenger door, waiting.

"It's open," he said as he slid into the driver's seat.

Chivalry was good and truly dead. She hadn't expected him to open her door or anything, but he could have at least put her overnight bag in the back for her.

Scowling she yanked open the door, swung her bag between the seats, almost hitting him in the face, and dropped it on the backseat.

He turned the key in the ignition and glanced in the rear-view mirror, then at her. "Is he, uh, here?"

"Is who here?" She knew exactly what he was asking but she liked making him squirm.

It was obvious he was really bugged out about Gabe. All the ghosts, really. It was refreshing to be the one in charge of the situation for once.

"You know. The ghost," he whispered.

"His hearing seems to be excellent so whispering wouldn't help if he were here, which he isn't."

Liam frowned. "Wait. Why not? Don't we need him to find the treasure?"

"He told me everything we'll need. He talked for like an hour and I took copious notes. Besides that, he's not sure he can come with us."

"What do you mean he's not sure?"

"He's still new at being a ghost." Hence his continued forgetting he can't lean on things and falling through them. "But he thinks he can't travel too far from his body. He tried walking across the bridge over the river and said he couldn't make it to the other side. It felt as if something was pushing against him. Holding him back."

Liam spread his hands. "Then we could have brought his body with us."

"Eew. No." She sent him a glare.

"Oh, so you're fine being best friends with a ghost but you're afraid of a body?"

"So you have no trouble carving up cadavers but you're afraid of a ghost?" she countered.

"Not afraid. Just... disturbed. It's not normal."

"Judging by the depth and breadth of the ghost population in this town, I'm afraid it's more normal than we ever imagined."

He gave a little shiver at that idea before his gaze connected with hers. "Did any come with your place? The depot looks pretty old."

"Inside, no. Thank God. But a guy dressed like he's heading to a day of work on the train walks past at the same time every morning and every evening. And the ghosts from town can come inside, except Gabe asked them not to."

"And they listened?"

She shrugged. "So far."

"Even though he's the new guy?"

"Yeah. I guess." She wasn't really up on the social hierarchy of ghosts. Maybe the newly dead where the upper echelon. Who knew?

"Let's hope your notes are good enough and this isn't a waste of a trip."

"Thanks for the confidence."

"Don't blame me. The one guy who came close to finding this treasure isn't here. And it's not like you can call him on your cell." He frowned. "You can't, can you?"

"I—Actually, I don't know. I mean he wouldn't be able to hit a button to answer the call, but I wonder... If I was talking to Harper or Jules on speaker phone and Gabe spoke, why wouldn't I be able to hear him? Maybe we can talk to him." As long as she could convince Jules or Harper to put her on speaker and convey to Gabe what she wanted to ask without sounding insane.

"Except you can't call either one of them and ask them to put Gabe on the line because you lied to them. They don't know you can see ghosts, do they?" Liam asked, echoing her own concern.

"No. Not yet." Maybe not ever. She was still wrapping her head around this herself.

"So if you didn't tell them, who else knows?"

"You," she answered.

"Me? Just me?" His eyes widened.

She nodded. "Just you."

He shot her a sideways glance as he pulled onto the highway and merged into traffic, all two cars of it.

"Why just me?" he asked once they were safely in the center lane with cruise control set.

"I guess I care too much about what everyone else will think of me."

"But you don't care what I think?" he asked.

"Correct."

He cocked up a brow, shot her a glance then said, "All right."

"All right? You're not mad?" she asked.

"Nope. I don't care what anyone thinks about me either."

A laugh she couldn't control escaped her. She covered her mouth then shot him a glance. "Sorry. But that's good you don't care."

"And why is that?"

"Because I've heard you're a hit man, a serial killer, a Navy SEAL, a private investigator and... Oh, yeah. A mercenary for hire."

He bobbed his head. "I can accept that. Except I was Army not Navy," he said with pride before mumbling, "Navy. Hmph. No way."

"So, what made you want to work with cadavers? It seems pretty far flung from being in the Army."

"Not at all. I was a medic when I was in. When I got out I used my college benefit to start on my medical degree."

"Why didn't you finish? Getting your medical degree?"

He sent her a sideways glance. "I finished."

"Then why are you working with bodies instead of live patients?"

"I don't like people enough to work with them for the next thirty years."

"Yeah. That tracks," she mumbled.

"And the only way I can find out how to prevent traumatic brain injury and learn how it relates to depression and the high rate of veteran suicide is to look at the brain. Literally look at it. That's easier after death."

Dammit. Was this people-hating, insulting man really a nice guy? Working to try to prevent veterans' suicides and brain issues?

"But wait. If you're studying brain damage in the

cadavers, why did you choose Gabe's body? And the two old ladies?"

"First, you take what you can get. Getting a cadaver isn't like ordering off a Chinese food menu."

Natalie found that image disturbing, but the mention of food also made her hungry. She should have packed a snack.

"And, your friend Gabe did have brain damage," he continued.

"Really? But he was stabbed."

"The damage wasn't from his death. It was from when he was alive. I don't know what he did in life since he came to me as a John Doe, but he's got signs of long-term brain trauma."

"Long term. Like he was a boxer maybe?" she asked.

"Does he look to you like he was a boxer?"

"No. He looks like Indiana Jones."

"Well, since you've got this new power and all, maybe you could ask him for me. Find out what he used to do that could have damaged his brain. If he played football. Or was in the military. But no. If he'd been military they'd have his fingerprints on file and he wouldn't be a John Doe. I'm thinking football."

"I'll ask for you as soon as we get home."

"What do you think he's doing there with us gone?"

Liam asked, uncharacteristically concerned about someone other than himself.

Although she couldn't really think about him like a bad guy anymore. He'd dedicated his life to helping those with brain injuries. Getting used to him not being the villain was going to take some time.

"I think he'll hang around my shop with Harper and Julia. Then, after closing, he might go to the cemetery. Gunshot wound guy invited him over to visit."

Liam cursed beneath his breath. "Too fucking weird."

She shrugged. "I guess. But it makes sense they'd enjoy some of the same things we do. They're just people. Only they're dead."

He shot her a glance. "If you say so."

"You're just upset because you've been carving up walking talking sentient beings like they're a Thanksgiving turkey."

His gaze shot sideways again before he said, "You're not wrong."

Chapter Fifteen

"This is it?" Natalie asked, peering through the windshield of Liam's Jeep at the square building with the sign that read *Town Hall*.

Liam nodded. "The person I talked to in Albany was helpful. I have the complete timeline for the cadaver—uh, I mean Gabe. The local Pine Plains police department got routed to the scene by the 9-1-1 operator. They brought in the ME. Uh, that's the medical examiner."

"I know what ME means." She scowled. She watched television. She knew things.

"Fine. So after enough time passed with no identification and no one claiming the body, they would have to declare him a John Doe. That's when the morgue contacted the donation center in Albany to take the body. They had it until I requested it—him."

This town was small. So, she guessed, was the police department. The fact the police operated out of an office located in the Town Hall proved that.

No wonder Gabe had become a John Doe.

"Did the people in Albany wonder why you were asking so many questions?"

"I didn't offer and they didn't ask. Although I did have my lie ready just in case."

Interested, she turned in her seat to face him. "Oh, please, do tell. I need to hear this. What were you going to say?"

Dark brows knit above his eyes. "Why do you need to know?"

"Because I've been scrambling for believable lies for days now." Ever since that day after the interview.

Having become a bit of a fib aficionado herself, it would be interesting to hear someone else's attempts to not reveal her new ability to communicate with the dead. Or in this case, the murdered.

He drew in a breath and she tried not to stare at the pecs beneath his Human Institute logo shirt.

"I was going to say I was researching the effects of living in different regions of the United States on the body, so I needed to know where it—*he* originated from."

Liam was obviously trying to wrap his head around Gabe not being an *it* or a *body* but actually a person with a name. Trying, but also mostly failing.

Of course, he was still new at this ghost stuff. She'd had days ahead of him to get used to it all.

"Not bad," she nodded then glanced at the building that housed the Pine Plains police department. "Got any ideas how we can reveal their John Doe's identity without getting locked up in a padded cell?"

Lips pressed tight he sent her a sideways glance. "This one might be a little harder. But I do have one idea."

"Really? What?"

He drew in another chest-expanding breath which she valiantly did not stare at then finally said, "What if I said we ran him through facial recognition and cross referenced it with missing persons during the same time period our cadaver was killed?"

Her eyes widened. "That's brilliant."

"Is it? Because I don't know if Gabe was reported as a missing person. What if he was a loner? He was traveling in pursuit of this treasure. He might have been thousands of miles from home when he was killed. Hell, he could live in a tent like a nomad for all we know. His name seems kind of common so I'm not sure even a search online would help."

"I think I have something that might help." She reached for her bag and took out a fat file folder.

"What's that?"

"My notes."

His brow rose, but he didn't comment. She had no time to wonder if he was judging her for her excessive note taking or not.

"Gabe has some gaps in his memory—the ghosts believe dying does that to you—but he remembered a lot. Maybe something in here might be helpful."

"He got a family?" Liam asked, eyeing the folder in her hand.

She shook her head. "Only child. Parents are dead. There's one cousin on his mom's side and her kids and grandkids, who he never met."

"Friends?"

She cringed. "Yes. Kind of. More like online associates. Not really close enough to notice him missing."

Liam let out a breath. "What about his house or apartment? Is there a neighbor? Landlord? Mortgage?"

"Yes. He rented an apartment and he remembered his address." She finally found the correct paper and glanced up. "What if we call his landlord? Say we've been trying to get in touch with him. We're concerned since we haven't been able to and we thought that something bad might have happened to him."

"You have the landlord's name?"

"No. But shouldn't public tax records give us the name of the owner of the building?"

"I guess it's worth a try." He looked out the window. "We probably shouldn't be conducting our research in the car in view of the police station. It looks suspicious."

"You're right." She slumped back. "By the time we get our facts straight, talk to the cops, hopefully grab something to eat, then do our own recon of the area—"

"Recon?"

"Shush... After doing all that it'll be getting late. Too late to drive back tonight. We planned and packed for at least an overnight trip. Maybe we should find a hotel now, one with WiFi. We can check in, set up a command center. Do our research, then come back here to the cops."

"Fine." He threw the Jeep into gear and pulled slowly away from the station. "Let's go find ourselves a *command center* for our *recon*."

"I'm sorry we can't all be war-hardened warriors and Silver Star medal recipients such as yourself." At her comment his gaze shot sideways. His hands tightened on the steering wheel.

"I never said I got the Silver Star." His eyes flicked wide before narrowing as he glared at her and asked, "Gabe?"

"Gabe," she confirmed. "He went through your stuff."

"I'm looking into an exorcism the minute we get back."

"What? No. That'll be like murdering him all over again."

"Maybe it just sends him to heaven or let's him go to eternal peace."

"You don't know that's what happens."

"You don't know that's *not* what happens."

"I'm not letting you harm Gabe."

"Then you'd better warn your new dead friend to stop snooping in my private life then reporting what he finds to everyone."

"Everyone." She snorted. "Anyone he talks to is dead except for me so..."

"So you're fine with him spying on you? You don't think he's sneaking around watching you shower and dress? How are you going to feel when you bring a guy home and Gabe gets his own live action sex show?"

"Ick. Stop. I'm sure he wouldn't—" The memory of gunshot wound guy peeping on the cemetery's new neighbor skidded into her mind and she wasn't so sure.

"Natalie. He's a ghost. What else does he have to do? What other enjoyment does he have? He can't eat. Does he even sleep?"

"I left the television on for him." She did try to be a good ghost host.

Liam snorted. "Great. But I hope he likes what's playing since he can't change the channel."

A hotel with a sign for cheap rates, free breakfast and WiFi came into view.

Liam swung into the parking lot. "Here we are. Command central. And doesn't it look lovely? Five stars. Can't wait to see that free breakfast."

He cut the engine and swung open the driver's side door. "Ready?"

Ready for an overnight road trip with Liam, who both tempted and annoyed her in almost equal amounts? Not even close.

Chapter Sixteen

Standing next to Liam and the counter—
both of which were so tall they made her feel small—
Natalie couldn't believe her ears.

"What do you mean there's only one room?" she
asked.

How could so many people possibly want to stay in
Pine Plains, New York in this cheap roadside motel that
it was almost completely full?

The front desk clerk shrugged. "It's graduation
weekend. If you'd made a reservation..."

"Is there another hotel nearby?" Liam asked.

"There's the Inn at Pine Plains not too far away. And
the Alander. They *might* have vacancies but no
guarantee. You'll have to call."

Natalie searched on her phone and almost swallowed

her tongue when she saw the prices. The two other places the clerk had suggested were over two hundred a night. Compared to here, which was eighty-four dollars per night and included free breakfast.

Even though she was planning on only paying for her own room, and not Liam's too since it had been his own idea to come, that was still a big chunk of change. Especially given her current financial position. And what if they ended up staying for two nights?

Liam leaned over to glance at what had her rapt on her cell phone's screen. His gaze moved from the rate amounts on the display to the expression on her face.

He turned back to the clerk. "We'll take the one room."

Her gaze whipped up to him. Them? Stay together? In one room?

"Put it on there." He tossed his credit card on the counter and glanced at Natalie. "It'll be fine."

She hadn't had time to voice her opinion or her objection yet, but apparently her face had done it for her and he knew she had concerns.

But he was paying so... She swallowed and managed a, "Mm-hm."

It was a good thing Gabe wasn't here to see this. He'd definitely have had plenty of comments about the situation. He always had comments about everything.

The clerk directed them where to park and gave them keys then it was time to grab the bags and head to the door of their room. The room they'd be sharing for the night. Together in good old room number fourteen —even though it was between rooms twelve and fifteen so technically it was room thirteen.

Yup. The way her luck had been running lately, that tracked.

As Liam fished one keycard out of the tiny cardboard envelope he glanced down at her next to him. "You should have told me money was tight."

Her gaze whipped to him. "What? It's not—"

He cocked up a brow.

She caved under the pressure of that brow. "Fine. It is. How did you know?"

"You don't exactly have a poker face."

"Never said I did," she mumbled with a pout. "I'll pay you back."

"No, you won't."

Rude Liam she could take. Smart ass Liam too. But Liam full of pity—for her—was unbearable.

Scowling, she knew the right thing to do was to thank him, even though she hadn't asked him to pay in the first place and had offered to pay him back.

"Thank you for paying for the room," she mumbled

pretty sure that her feelings on the whole matter must have been clear to him in her expression.

He tilted his head. "Don't thank me yet. It could be a shit hole. Besides, I invited myself along on this trip. I can pay for the room I'm going to sleep in. And when we find the buried treasure, I'll be expecting my share."

Treasure. Yeah, right. "You really think there's anything to find?"

"Why not? Stranger things have happened." He shrugged.

She'd come for Gabe, not for treasure. To give him the justice he deserved.

No. She didn't really believe she would be able to solve his murder over the next two days—if ever. But by giving the police the information they hadn't had when they'd declared him a John Doe, maybe the authorities could find his killer.

Whatever their respective reasons for being there, his pity still stung.

"Business is picking up," she said bringing them back to the point about her being *temporarily* strapped for cash. "It just took a bigger investment than I anticipated to get the shop up and running."

Filling the store's shelves alone cost a small fortune.

"All the more reason to find the treasure." He shot

her a grin as he shoved the card in the slot and the lock disengaged with a beep.

He swung the door wide and stood, blocking her view and her entrance to the room.

"What?" she asked, trying to see around him.

He angled his body so she could see past him into the room... where there was only one bed.

Her eyes widened.

"It'll be fine for one night," he said, striding inside and planting his bag on top of the dresser.

What did that mean? Was he going to sleep on the floor and give her the bed?

She followed him inside though with a lot less enthusiasm, eyeballing the thin threadbare dark blue carpet that could hide any number of horrors. Dirt. Stains. Bugs. Bodily fluids.

No way was she sleeping on the floor and she couldn't expect him to either. Especially since he'd paid the bill.

She looked toward the bed, evaluating the size since it looked like they'd be sharing it. At least it was big. It took up the majority of the floorspace in the room.

"Let's see those extensive notes of yours so we know where to look for that treasure."

Bag still in her hand as she wondered where the cleanest and most bug free place to set it down was, she spun to face Liam. "Aren't we going to get the landlord's name and number first, call and then go back to the police station?"

"There's time for that. Let's see what good old Gabe had to say about the location first."

"Fine." Scowling, she handed over the folder to him, keeping the page with the address for herself.

He could delve into Gabe's long-winded ramblings about gangsters, whisky and Prohibition. She was going online to find that landlord's name.

The Mudville locals' theory that Liam was a mercenary was starting to seem more plausible as it seemed the only thing he was interested in was the treasure. Not justice for the man who'd possibly died because of it.

Her change of heart about him being a good guy based on their conversation in the car had reversed one more time. She was back to viewing him as a hot but not so nice guy. The kind of person she didn't want as a friend. The kind of man she'd never want to date.

Good. That would make sleeping next to his hot hard body in the same bed much easier tonight.

Probably.

Chapter Seventeen

Sitting in the cheap hotel room with one bed and one chair—eighty-four dollars a night didn't get a guest many furnishings—Natalie channeled every FBI, CIA or police procedural show and movie she'd ever seen and dove into the task of researching Gabe's landlord in Ohio.

The only thing missing from the scene was some bad coffee and a murder-board. The first item would be easy enough to obtain. The second, not so much.

She'd have to make do with her laptop propped on the nightstand, the free WiFi and the legal pad scrawled with notes next to her.

Gabe had been dead long enough someone should have noticed he was behind on rent. But that person might have just slapped an eviction notice on the door, waited the required amount of time, then removed his belongings. Lack of payment did not mean anyone filed a missing person's report.

On the bed, shoes kicked off, sprawled Liam, frowning at a page of her notes. "Your handwriting is atrocious. And I'm a doctor—the profession legendary for bad handwriting."

"Deal with it." She couldn't hold his hand and decipher her notes for him, which were written perfectly legibly in her opinion. She had work to do.

First, find the name of the owner of the building where he lived in the suburbs of Cleveland. Step one to accomplish that—the online Chagrin Falls, Ohio property tax records.

Chagrin. She typed that name into the search field along with the words property records while thinking it was a most unfortunate name for a town.

As the search results populated her screen she shot a glance at Liam, frowning while deep into his reading the notes from Gabe. At least he was quiet so she could do what they'd come here to do. Help Gabe.

Her Zillow obsession had taught her it was pretty easy to discover who owned a property. All she needed was the address and the internet. *Except* in the cases when the owner was listed as a corporation, apparently, which was exactly the situation she faced now.

She let out a huff, which unfortunately drew Liam's attention. "Problem?"

"No. No problem. Just a roadblock. I'll get around it," she said with more confidence than she felt.

"All right," he said, going back to the file.

Determined, more to prove to Liam she could do what she said she would, she jumped through hoops and performed some major acrobatics online. Finally after more time than she liked, success.

She didn't find the name of Gabe's landlord, but she might have found the next best thing—his neighbor. In a duplex with only two tenants they had to know each other, right? She certainly hoped so as she tapped on the message button on the woman's Facebook profile.

Now came the really tricky part... asking for information without sounding like a stalker.

> Hi, Margot. You don't know me but I'm friends with your neighbor Gabe through an online group. No one in the group has heard from him lately and he's not answering any of my messages. Have you seen him lately? I'm concerned about him.

Natalie reviewed the lie-filled message.

This talking to ghosts stuff was tricky. There wasn't

much more she could say. If she truly were just a concerned online friend she wouldn't know anymore.

Of course, Gabe's neighbor could think she was a jilted lover or crazed stalker that Gabe was avoiding on purpose.

That was a risk, but maybe the message would at least make her realize she hadn't seen Gabe lately so she'd become concerned herself.

Staring at the screen, she waited for the little dots that indicated Margot was typing to appear. There weren't any. Not for a solid five minutes that seemed like more.

Finally, the dots appeared. Natalie leaned closer to the screen in anticipation until the message loaded.

How do you know Gabe again?

Natalie flashed back to her notes. The notes she would have loved to have next to her right now. Annoyed with Liam, she winged it and typed in a reply.

We met in a private group of whisky collectors. He's very knowledgable about rare and vintage bottles of whisky.

Natalie's hope began to fade as it took Margot a long time to reply. Finally she did.

> He does love to talk about old booze...

> I haven't seen him for a while but he travels a lot.

Phew. She could work with that. She had the timing of his death from the body donation place in Albany and she had Gabe's own words about where he'd been.

> Yes. Last I talked to him, he said he was going to New York to check out some distillery. He said he'd report back to us about the quality of the whisky. But that was a while ago and no one in our group has heard from him since. That's why I'm worried something happened to him. What if he had a car accident or something?

She was really throwing the bull shit now. She could only hope it would work.

My boyfriend and I were out of town
for a while and we don't see Gabe all
that often. But now that you mention
it, people come through the complex
every weekend and hang food
delivery menus on our doors. His
door has a whole bunch of them.

Yes! Finally. Natalie decided it was time to close the deal.

I'm REALLY concerned something
happened to him. Maybe you should
report him as a missing person to the
police?

I don't know… What if nothing is
wrong? He might get upset I called
the police.

Natalie couldn't tell her Gabe wasn't going to get upset because he was dead. She scrambled for another tactic.

Do you have his landlord's phone
number? I could call him. Maybe he
heard from Gabe? If something bad
happened the landlord might know.

I guess so. OK. I'll give you our landlord's number but don't tell him you got it from me. He's not a very nice person.

Please don't tell him I said that!

Wouldn't dream of it. Your secret is safe with me.

A phone number and an email address with the landlord's name came through in the next message and after replying with an exclamation point-laden *thank you*, Natalie squinted at the hieroglyphics she'd scribbled on her pad. The notes she'd taken about their conversation. Fine. Maybe her penmanship could use a little work, but she'd been shaking as she got closer to helping Gabe.

Now all that was left was to call the landlord and get him to report his tenant missing...

Except he didn't answer.

Reporting a murder victim who was a John Doe was proving harder than she'd imagined it would be. They should show more about this annoying part of murder investigations on television. It would be more realistic.

She left a message that she hoped sounded convincing, adding her cell number and a request he call her back before disconnecting.

What now? Maybe the local newspaper archives? Would they have posted about finding an unidentified body? Would there be a picture so she could claim to recognize him? Probably not. That would be gruesome.

Maybe she could just go to the police and use the same missing friend story she'd given Margot. Say Gabe's last known location was here and did they have any reports of accidents... or bodies.

Yeah, that didn't sound too off the wall. And what if they wanted proof of how she knew him? Or didn't believe her that he was actually missing?

Slumping back in her chair, she let out a sigh and once again drew Liam's attention.

"Happy now? You did your due diligence and called the landlord."

No, she was not happy.

She scowled at him. "It's not enough. We're no closer to telling the police their John Doe is Gabe. I can't count on either the landlord or the neighbor to file a missing person's report. And even if they do, it's still going to be hard to get the local police to connect a missing man in Ohio to their unidentified body in New York."

"Patience. Gabe's already dead. He can't get any deader. There's time."

She narrowed her eyes at him. Gabe might not be

deader but he was in a few more pieces than he used to be thanks to Doctor Death, who she'd be sharing a bed with tonight.

Besides, he was wrong about there being time. Was he too busy sawing up bodies to watch any police shows?

"The trail could go cold," she lectured. "The longer we wait, the more chance the killer could cover his tracks and get away. And besides, I could tell you to be patient too. This treasure has been hidden for a century. It's not going anywhere."

"I beg to differ. Gabe was looking for it. Possibly whoever killed him was also looking for it. Any number of people could be hot on the trail and close to finding it. We need to get out there now and start looking."

She rolled her eyes but gave in. Only because she had already done all she could on the Gabe front... for now.

"Fine." Although she hated to let him have his way, she stood and reached for the folder. "The hottest lead according to Gabe is the local distillery."

"Why the distillery? From what I found on Google, Dutch was supposed to have hidden the treasure near Phoenicia. We're like fifty miles from there."

"Are you going to believe Google or Gabe?" she asked.

He cocked up one brow but asked, "What exactly did Gabe say?"

"He thought the key is here in Pine Plains. And the fact he was killed here and not in Phoenicia supports the theory that this town is important. So I did a search and found a New York Times article about the distillery. Federal agents in 1932 called it one of the largest and most elaborate moonshine operations in this part of the country. But here's the best part, it's connected to a network of *hidden tunnels*."

"That in the Times article?" he asked.

She nodded.

"So *not* so hidden then," he pointed out.

"No. But what if there were more, maybe on the neighboring farms, undiscovered?"

"That what Gabe thinks?"

"Yes."

"So you want us to go trespassing looking for tunnels? Any chance that's what Gabe was doing when he got stabbed?" Liam asked, looking less enthusiastic about the treasure hunt now.

"He doesn't remember actually getting stabbed or even much of the time right before he died. Remember? I told you. He thinks it's some sort of side effect of the trauma of dying."

"Hmm." Liam got a faraway look in his eyes.

She shot him an accusatory glare. "You're thinking about his brain again, aren't you?"

"Yeah. Sorry. Okay, how about this? We start at the distillery. Learn what we can there. Then move on to other possibilities."

"All right," she agreed. It wasn't a great plan but at least it was a plan.

Chapter Eighteen

"So we take a tour of the historic distillery, then we'll go to the police station?" Natalie glanced sideways at Liam in the driver's seat as the Jeep whizzed past farmland that probably looked much like it had in the days of Dutch's association with the area.

"You want to go to the police before the landlord gets back to you? When you don't even know if the neighbor reported him missing yet?" He cocked up one brow ripe with skepticism. "We can go if you want, but if I were the one who had to explain that I knew the identity of a dead body without revealing it's because I talked to his ghost, I'd wait for a missing person's report to be filed at least."

He had a point. She hated that.

Giving in with a scowl, she said, "Fine. We'll wait."

At least he didn't rub it in that he was right. Probably because he was speeding toward the turn off, rather than slowing down to make the turn like a sane person would have.

Gabe was right. Hunting for treasure made people crazy. Crazy enough to kill him. Crazy enough for Liam to put them in mortal danger with his unsafe driving.

She braced one hand on the door armrest and delivered a pointed and judgmental glare at Liam... which he ignored as the Jeep bounced over the gravel driveway that would take them to the distillery.

He threw the Jeep into park and cut the engine. As he turned to glance at her, the energy radiated off him. "Ready?"

"You certainly are. Excited much?" she commented.

Green eyes glared at her from beneath lowered black brows. "The question is, why aren't you *more* excited? We're on a real-life treasure hunt. How many people can say that?"

"Living people? One less than before. There is the matter of Gabe's murder," she reminded him.

Getting killed while treasure hunting was a bit of an excitement killer, in her opinion.

"You're with me now. No one's going to kill you. Promise," he said with the snap of his seatbelt before he all but bolted out the door of the Jeep.

"Forgive me if I'm skeptical," she said with the release of her own belt.

Inside, the distillery was set up to be part tourist attraction, part tasting room-slash-drinking establishment, and part store where people could stock up on branded bottled *moonshine* to take home.

"Come on. The next tour is leaving. We have to get on it," Liam said as he wrapped an arm around her shoulders and motored her toward the tour group.

She had to take two quick steps to every one of his long ones.

Finally, when they'd caught up and joined the tail end of the group slowly shuffling behind the employee speaking up front, he slowed.

She eyed his hand on her shoulder. "What are you doing?"

He leaned low and said too close to her ear, "Couples are less suspicious. Now shush."

She didn't think she looked suspicious whether she was part of this sham couple or not, and she really didn't like being shushed by him or anyone, but she didn't argue. Instead she strained to listen to what the leader of the group said.

There could be clues all around them. Something that could help Gabe.

Liam, on the other hand, seemed to be looking

everywhere except at the tour guide. Not a surprise. Far be it from him to actually listen to someone else talk.

They moved from the well-lit public area of the distillery through a doorway and descended into the formerly secret tunnels used during Prohibition.

"This is more like it," Liam commented.

She took that as an opportunity to shush him this time as she listened to the names and dates their guide listed. The guide mentioned historical figures she was familiar with and others she hadn't heard of but Gabe probably had. She wished she had a notebook and pen to take notes for him.

Ooo. She did have her phone. There were apps for that.

She pulled the cell out of her bag and was about to try to locate a recording app while not completely missing what was being said when she saw him—a man standing off to the side.

He hadn't been with them on the tour. He wasn't wearing the logo shirt like the employees she'd seen. He was older, but not frail.

There was a toughness about him as he leaned against the wall, arms folded as he watched people go by. But not one person looked at him—and finally it hit her that was because *they* couldn't see him. But she could.

She reached out to grip Liam's forearm. He frowned down at her.

"Hang back," she whispered.

He slowed his pace then stopped. When the group had moved far enough away, he asked, "What's up?"

"Don't look but I think—we're not alone." She'd mouthed the last three words while facing him and away from the possible specter.

He frowned, then his eyes widened. "Oh. You mean...like at home?"

She nodded and held up one finger to indicate there was only one possible ghost there with them.

He leaned low and pressed his mouth to her ear. A shiver ran through her and she felt almost woozy from the heat of his lips against her.

"How about you ask him some questions?" Liam's whispered suggestion knocked her back to reality.

She pulled back and glared at him.

Was he crazy? Talking to Gabe was one thing. He was familiar. Like a friend. She trusted he'd never hurt her. In fact, he protected her privacy from the others.

But she didn't know what other ghosts were capable of.

No doubt not all were kind and gentle. Some had to be malevolent. At least they were if there was any truth to any of the stories ghost hunter reality shows or even movies were based on.

Could he hurt her? Was he capable? And what would he do once he knew she could hear and see him? She already knew ghosts liked to get way too close.

Afraid to speak lest she give away her ability, all she did was catch Liam's gaze with her own wide-eyed one and shake her head.

"You scared?"

"Yes." She nodded.

"But—"

She covered his mouth with her fingers. "Shh."

He rolled his eyes and pulled her hand away, keeping it held captive in his, which was completely distracting but not unpleasant. Comforting, actually.

"So you're just going to give up? Go home and tell poor murdered Gabe you can't help because you're too afraid?"

At the name Gabe, the man in the corner perked up. His gaze zeroed in on Liam, then moved to her.

"Shit," she breathed.

"What?"

"He heard you."

Apparently all spirits had no sense of propriety or personal space. The male moved closer, then closer still until Natalie had to pull her arms in front of herself, curling in her shoulders to avoid brushing up against the ghost.

"Is he right there? Next to you?" Liam asked.

She nodded.

"Okay. Enough. Dude. Back off and she'll be happy to listen to whatever you want to say. It's a pretty good deal since I'm thinking you don't get many living people who can see and hear you."

Liam was still directing his heroic monologue to the space next to her shoulder. But as soon as he'd addressed the spirit, it swooped backward, all the way to the wall of the tunnel.

"He moved," she told Liam, before she turned to the spirit. "Look. What he said is true. I can see you. If you talk I should be able to hear you too. And I'm happy to listen to whatever you want to say. But I'd really like to hear what you know about my friend Gabe. He was murdered—stabbed—we think nearby very recently and I promised him I'd try to find his killer."

The ghost snorted. "Not nearby. It all went down right here, doll." His voice was gruff. His speech akin to that of an old timey gangster from the movies.

Now that she thought about it, her life had become more and more like a movie lately.

"What do you mean, here?" she asked.

"Right here in the tunnels. Just about where you're

standing, then the killer dragged him off that-away." He tipped his chin toward where the tour group had gone.

"Are you sure?"

He was standing too closely again and as interested as she was in what he had to say, she had to take a step back. For her own sense of comfort. And her sanity.

"Yeah, I'm sure. I saw the whole thing," he reported.

She forgot about putting space between them at that and leaned forward. "You saw it?"

"Saw what?" Liam demanded. "What are you two talking about?"

"Gabe being stabbed." She glanced at Liam. "It happened here."

"Here, here?" Liam glanced at the dirt and stone floor, then up at her. "We need a black light. It'll show any traces of blood."

She waved away his amateur forensics and turned back to the ghost. "How did you know his name was Gabe? Did he talk to you—ghost-to-ghost—after he died?" she asked.

The spirit shook his head. "He was still alive and breathing when he dragged him away."

"You said *he*. So it was definitely a man who stabbed him?"

The ghost nodded. "Dames don't go for knives usually. Even the tough ones. It was a man for sure and he called your friend by name. Said, 'Hey, Gabe,' clear as day. And Gabe turned and said, 'What're you doing here?' The guy said something about following him and Gabe should know why. There was a lot more conversation. A bit of a tussle. Your friend turned to leave and the yellow-bellied coward grabbed the knife right out of the sheath on Gabe's belt and stabbed him in the back with it. Then he dragged him out of here."

"And no one saw?"

He shook his head. "The place was closed. I was the only one around to see. Knife must've gotten him in the lung. Poor bastard was gurgling. Probably drowned in his own blood."

The shock of that image had Natalie silent until she felt Liam's hand on her shoulder. "What?"

She drew in enough breath to say over the sound of her pounding heart, "Gabe knew his killer."

Liam blew out a curse beneath his breath.

They were closer to finding Gabe's killer than she ever believed they'd get. All because she'd spoken to this ghost, like Liam told her too—which stung. She *really* hated him being right.

"Thank you—um. I'm sorry. I don't know your name."

"What? You don't recognize me, doll?" he asked with a grin.

She shook her head. "Sorry. No. I'm not from around here. Oh, wait. Are you—you're not Dutch Schultz, are you?"

Was she speaking with the famous gangster? The man who knew exactly where the treasure would be? She couldn't believe her luck.

He laughed. "Hell no. I was just kidding you. I'm a nobody. And I happen to know Dutch moved a good amount of the hooch but he wasn't the mastermind behind the operation that everyone gives him credit for. That was Patrick Ryan, the owner of the farm. He was the brains behind it all. And he's the one that would have gone down for it after the bust in 1932. Except he had connections from being a former cop and all."

"Then who are you?"

"I worked here back then. During Patrick Ryan's time before he sold it. I bought the place thirty years later. That was in the late sixties after a bunch of owners had fucked it up. It was everything from a commune to a slaughterhouse before I got it."

"Wow," Natalie breathed.

She'd have never known. It had been brought back to its Prohibition glory today to draw in the tourists.

"Wow what?" Liam asked. "You have to get better about keeping me in the loop."

Ignoring him, the ghost continued, "Those other

owners never knew the secrets. Never found the rest of the tunnels or the storeroom. But I know. Charles Adams, at your service."

Natalie smiled. "Nice to meet you, Charles."

"Who the hell is Charles?" Liam hissed from just behind her.

"Who's this cake-eater?" Charles lifted a chin toward Liam.

"A pain in my neck," she mumbled.

"He carries himself like a G-man." Charles eyed Liam with a suspicious stare. "He a fed?"

"He's former military. And now he's a doctor of sorts, I guess. Not a…G-man or a fed. I promise."

He nodded. "Good. Never trust a fed."

"I'm waiting for an answer," Liam said while actually tapping his foot. "And I'm not a *doctor of sorts*. I'm actually a doctor. When are you going to believe that? Do I need to show you my med school diploma?"

She drew in a breath. "*Doctor* William Walsh, meet Charles Adams. He worked here for the original owner of the distillery, Patrick Ryan."

"As in during Prohibition?" Liam stared at her.

"Wouldn't have been much money in cooking up and smuggling moonshine if it hadn't been during Prohibition, now would it?" Charles said snarkily.

"Yes," she answered Liam and ignored the ghost with the attitude.

"Then why haven't you asked him about the treasure? If it's here, won't he know?"

Liam did have a point. She'd been distracted with solving the murder—*her* reason for being here. But the treasure did seem to be connected to the murder. And as long as they were here, she might as well ask.

"Did you ever hear anything about Dutch Schultz burying gold, diamonds and cash somewhere around here?"

"That was the rumor. Sure." Charles nodded.

"Rumor? You don't believe it?" she asked.

He shrugged. "It wouldn't do much good to hide the loot then run your mouth off. If he did hide anything around here, why would he tell everybody about it? Nah. Dutch could be a cocky bastard but he wasn't that dumb."

She nodded in agreement with what Charles said as Liam prodded her in the side with two pointy fingers.

"He doesn't think it's here," she said to appease him before he poked her again.

Liam visibly deflated. She couldn't deal with him now since she heard the tour coming back in their direction.

"We're going to have to go. But you've been very helpful. Thank you so much," she said to Charles.

"No problem, doll."

She turned, planning to rejoin the group when they got close enough, when a thought struck her and she pivoted back. "Wait. Can you leave here? You're not trapped in the tunnels are you?"

"Hell, no. I can go all over the property. But it's most fun to scare the tourists down here." He grinned.

She couldn't help but smile. "Have fun, Charles."

Turning back to Liam, she saw his unhappy expression as he mumbled, "I don't like being on the outside looking in."

Finally, payback for all of his rude, not to mention antisocial behavior.

"Sorry," she said with not much sympathy before flouncing her way back to the main group.

Chapter Nineteen

"THERE HAS TO BE MORE," LIAM INSISTED while the hamburger poised in his hand dripped grease into the take-out container below it.

"I told you every word Charles said to me."

Liam rolled his eyes. "You can't remember every word."

"Sure I can. I have a very good memory," Natalie lied.

She hoped he didn't ask her to remember what she'd had for dinner last night because she had no idea. But when it came to important things, like ghosts talking about witnessing murders, a person tended to remember.

Liam shook his head. "I don't believe there's no treasure. First of all, rumors have to start somewhere.

From some ounce of truth. Second, someone killed Gabe over this treasure."

"That doesn't mean it wasn't some crazy treasure obsessed person willing to kill over just a rumor." She looked pointedly at Liam, who had definitely become treasure obsessed. "What's with you and the treasure anyway? Do you need money?"

If so, she could relate. She too had taken on a piece of real estate that had turned into a money pit. Old buildings might sell for cheap, but the real cost was in the renovation and maintenance. She'd learned that too late.

She could only imagine what Liam's building was like inside and how much work he was doing to turn it into an operating lab.

He set down the remaining piece of his burger with a sigh. "You ever hear of the Treasure of Nimrud."

"No. Wait. Is it a book? Or was it a movie?"

He shook his head. "It's all the gold and jewels and artifacts that were discovered in some ancient queen's tomb in the late eighties. It was called the greatest discovery since King Tut. It's considered priceless and it all disappeared from the Iraq Museum. I was stationed in Baghdad with my unit so we were definitely aware of the treasure."

"And you searched for it," she guessed.

"Actually the treasure of Nimrud was found but we knew there was still a lot of Saddam Hussein's gold hidden somewhere. Probably right in the city. My buddy and I used to joke about searching for it and what we'd do if we ever found it. Fantasy stuff, you know. I wanted to buy an island. He wanted to open a casino..." His voice trailed off.

"Well maybe after we figure out who Gabe's killer is you and your buddy can pick up Gabe's search for this treasure."

The search for Dutch's treasure might have already proven dangerous—at least to Gabe—but she had to think it was safer than going to Iraq.

"My friend...died."

"Oh." That she hadn't expected. "I'm sorry."

He responded with barely a nod before standing. "I'm taking a shower."

"Okay." She watched him walk away as questions swirled in her brain. Questions about the circumstances of his friend's death. About what else Liam had gone through in his years of service. Questions she knew she'd never ask. And even if she did, she doubted he'd answer.

The conversation, as short as it had been, did maybe explain one thing. Why Liam was obsessed with this treasure. He was pursuing the dream he and his buddy shared. Carrying on the torch his friend couldn't.

She supposed she had to respect that. She could even understand it. Finding Dutch's stash would be cool. Even if they did donate it all to a museum or whatever she wouldn't mind finding it. The publicity might even help the shop.

But first, Gabe's murder... That was the priority.

Shoving the last piece of her chicken sandwich into her mouth, she chewed while she logged into her email. Still no answer from the landlord. And there'd been no phone call or text either.

If he didn't get back to them soon, they would have no evidence that Gabe was missing to bring to the local police. And how in the world was she going to get the police to look in the tunnels for blood? The killer had moved the body so it wasn't found there.

She was still making her head spin with circular arguments about how she could or could not involve the police when the bathroom door opened and Liam emerged wearing nothing but a towel around his hips.

Then there were no more thoughts of tunnels or police.

Holy hell!

He might be a doctor—or so he said—but he was built more like an Olympic athlete. All lean muscles and that vee that guys got from having wide shoulders and a narrow waist.

"Sorry. I forgot to grab clean clothes before I went in." He glanced at her from beneath the fall of wet hair hanging low over his eyes.

She swallowed hard and tried to find words as he turned to dig through is bag.

"Uh, that's fine. No biggie. Nothing I haven't seen before." She let out a manic sounding laugh.

His brows rose as his gaze shot to her briefly but he didn't comment as he continued to paw—one handed as he held the towel with the other—through the clothes in his bag.

Grabbing a pair of shorts and a T-shirt while still holding that precariously poised towel with his other hand, he went back into the bathroom.

"I'll be out in a second then the shower is all yours."

"Oh sure. Yeah. Thanks." The door closed again and she let out a breath.

She'd shower. And after that... Swallowing hard she glanced at the one and only bed in the room.

Chapter Twenty

NATALIE WOKE SLOWLY. HER BRAIN SEEMED TO take longer than her body to function.

She opened her eyes and tried to place where she was. The room was still dark but as her eyes adjusted, cheap ugly hotel furniture in the small square room came into focus.

The motel. With Liam. Together. In the one and only bed.

Holy shit.

She'd actually slept but now she was very much awake...and so was one particular part of Liam. That part was currently poking her in the butt.

Afraid to move, afraid to breathe, she froze, her body stiff... and that wasn't the only thing that was stiff in that bed.

She should slide off the mattress and slip out of bed. That was the only thing she could do. She could probably make her getaway and not wake him. He was breathing the deep steady breaths of sleep.

There was nothing to panic about. Morning wood was just a reflex, right? He had no control of it. It had nothing to do with her.

Unconscious as he was, he probably didn't even know she was there—

One thick heavy arm flopped over her.

She held her breath and listened as his breathing continued in a deep steady in-and-out cadence.

Then he moaned, soft, low and pulled her back. Tighter against him.

Now what?

She listened but no longer heard the telltale steady breaths of sleep. Was he awake? Did he know what he was doing? And what if he did?

What if he wanted her...as much as she was starting to have to admit that she wanted him too?

She had to know.

Slowly she rolled over onto her back. That put her face right next to his. His eyes were closed until suddenly they weren't.

They opened and then they flew open farther.

"Jesus. Shit. Natalie. I'm sorry." He started to

withdraw his arm from where it rested across her stomach.

That caused his fingers to brush the bare skin where her T-shirt had ridden up. Where it didn't reach the waist of the cotton shorts she'd slept in. She drew in a sharp breath at the contact as goose bumps rose on her skin.

She fell into his gaze as his eyes connected with hers. Until his gaze dropped to her mouth as she parted her lips on an inhale.

He cocked up a brow. "Maybe I'm not so sorry."

His gaze locked onto hers, he leaned in just a bit.

She didn't back up. She might have even let out the tiniest whimper.

He blew out a cuss then closed in on her and his lips covered hers.

It had been a long time since she'd had a man in her bed. That was her only explanation for how her leg ended up thrown over his hips as she pressed her core against the hard length barely contained by his shorts.

The kiss was damn near perfect. No cringe-worthy crashing of teeth. No painful, embarrassing smashing of noses. Just the right amount of moisture.

And when he thrust his tongue between her lips she felt it all the way to her core.

Since the first words he'd ever spoken to her, Liam

had been more likely than not to annoy her when he opened his mouth to speak. But as he kissed her there was no denying he had an exceptionally talented tongue.

It seemed he wasn't unaffected by the amazing joining of their mouths either. She felt his hard-on flex against her, almost keeping time with the thrusts of his tongue as he loved her mouth.

And all of this amazingness was with their clothes still on. She could only barely begin to imagine what he could do to her without the layers of restrictive fabric between them. As he reached down and shoved her shirt up, it looked as if she was about to find out.

His hand was warm and the air conditioning cold against her newly exposed skin as he shoved her shirt higher before breaking the kiss long enough to tug it over her head.

Dipping his head low, he popped one breast out of the top of her sleeping bralette then latched onto her nipple. The heat combined with the pull of the suction of his mouth had the long-ignored muscles inside her clenching. It wrenched a long low sound of pleasure from her that Liam echoed with a semi-feral groan.

Rolling her onto her back, he slid his hand down her stomach and beneath the elastic waistband of her shorts. He moved lower until he hit the spot she needed him most.

"So wet," he growled.

"Mmm," she managed as she let her legs fall farther apart.

"Want this," he mumbled as his finger dipped inside her.

"Mm-hm," she agreed.

He hissed air in between his teeth as his finger worked her and she replied with a squeak of pleasure at least two octaves higher than her usual voice.

As far as conversations went it wasn't much, which was probably a good thing since conversations between them were usually like oil and water. But the brief interaction was enough for Liam to spring into action.

He yanked her shorts down her legs, tossing them aside before he dove headfirst between her thighs.

The heat of his mouth on her core had her eyes slamming shut as her lips opened on a gasp. His fingers proved as talented as his tongue and the two combined were mind-blowingly good.

Liam's fingers hit a spot inside her that had her hips lifting and her breath coming faster. The pleasure ramped up along with the sound of her cries. She tangled her fingers in his hair and pressed his mouth tighter against her.

As wave after wave of the orgasm broke over her, she pried open her eyes just enough to see the top of his dark head—and the dead people standing behind him.

No!

No-no-no-no-no-no. Not now. Please.

Her current reality was far worse than the proverbial nightmare about going to school naked. She felt like an exhibitionist. She slammed her eyes closed and willed them away.

Pretend they're not there.

Why not? Ghosts had probably been watching her since the very first time her very first boyfriend slipped his hand under her shirt.

Her reasoning seemed sound but that didn't help with the distraction. Ghosts and orgasms didn't mix. Their presence put a halt to any afterglow she might have enjoyed.

Blissfully unaware—like she wished she were—Liam rolled off her. He shoved his shorts down his legs and all the way off, then he was back between her thighs.

"Ooo. Big boys about to go in bareback," the young male dressed like it was the 1950s narrated.

"Maybe she's on birth control," the old woman suggested.

The male snorted. "Or maybe he doesn't care."

Damn them for being here and ruining this moment, but the ghosts were right. Liam was about to slide that big, beautiful hard length inside her and oh how she wanted him to. But it had been so long since she'd had a serious boyfriend, she hadn't worried about birth control in years.

"Birth control?" she asked.

"Vasectomy," he answered before sliding all the way in on a single thrust with a loud groan.

"Oh. Good one. Never would have guessed that," the guy said.

"It's nice to see men taking responsibility for family planning nowadays," the woman agreed.

"Shhh," Natalie said as she tried to concentrate.

"Don't give a fuck who hears us," Liam grunted an answer even though her comment hadn't been meant for him.

With two hands beneath her, he lifted her hips, and set a pace that had her almost forgetting they weren't alone. Almost.

As Liam's grunts and thrusts both quickened, culminating in his back bowing and vocal orgasm, the applause from their unwelcome audience was a very real reminder they weren't alone.

Liam collapsed over her as she tried not to make eye contact with the visitors. If she wanted them to leave—and leave her alone—they couldn't know she could see them.

"Hey, want to see if room seven is still watching porn?" the young guy asked.

The old lady shrugged. "Sure." Then the surreal duo exited through the wall.

Natalie let out a breath.

Liam lifted his head from the pillow and frowned.

"What's wrong?" His eyes widened. "Did you not want to do that?"

"No. I mean yes. I wanted to."

"Then why do you look...like you've seen a ghost. Fuck." He ran a hand over his face. "You did, didn't you?"

She'd seen in his expression the moment the realization had hit him and he wasn't happy about it. "Um. Yes?"

"Shit. Why didn't you tell me?" He sat up completely, covering himself with the sheet.

"We were pretty well into it when they came in."

"They? How many were there?"

"Two," she answered and waited for him to react.

He blew out a cuss. "They still here?"

She very happily answered, "No."

Shaking his head, he said, "Being with you is certainly an experience."

She wasn't sure that was a compliment.

Chapter Twenty-One

"So you really think we shouldn't go to the police?" Natalie asked.

They'd checked out of their room in the motel after a not great but free continental breakfast and were navigating their way to the entrance to the highway.

Sex with Liam aside, the trip felt like a failure.

Yes, she'd gotten good information from Charles at the distillery, but the police still didn't know Gabe was their John Doe.

"Did the landlord get back to you?" Liam asked with quite an attitude in his tone.

"No." And he knew that so his question had obviously been rhetorical. Just to prove a point.

"And did the neighbor file a missing person's report?" he asked.

"I don't know." Something he also knew.

"Then what do you think?" he asked with evident attitude.

She screwed up her mouth. "You're grumpier than usual."

"Forgive me if I don't like being the unwitting star in the latest live-action ghost porn," he spat.

That's what he was mad about?

She rolled her eyes at his extreme sensitivity. "Hey. It's no picnic for me either, you know. I'm the one who can actually see and hear them."

"And yet you chose not to tell me they were there until *after*."

"I told you I didn't see them until we were pretty far into it. If it helps any, your grand finale got applause."

He looked less than pleased as he shot her a sideways glare. "You're not joking, are you?"

She sighed. "I wish I were."

He shook his head. "How am I supposed to live with this? Now I will always wonder for the rest of my life how many people are watching me fuck."

"I'm sorry. I wish I'd never gotten electrocuted. I wish I'd never started to see dead people. But there's nothing I can do about it. Okay?" Her voice broke on the last word as she wondered the same thing—how was she supposed to live like this?

Judging by Liam's reaction to her ghostly encounters, her future was becoming clear. And it wasn't good.

She'd have to lie to everyone she knew and loved. Her friends. Her family. Anyone she dated. Even anyone she, by some miracle, married.

They'd all have to be kept in the dark to spare them the horrors of the reality she now dealt with every moment of every day.

He glanced over and scowled as the first tear streamed down her cheek. "Don't you dare cry."

"Don't tell me what to do," she squeaked as more tears fell, fast and furious, in spite of his order.

He cussed and pulled over onto the shoulder. After shifting into park, he turned to face her. "All right. Go ahead. Get it over with so we can get on the road."

The reason for his choice to work with cadavers rather than live patients was becoming clearer. His bedside manner sucked. He'd obviously made the right choice.

"You're really horrible at this comforting stuff. You know that?" Her voice so high she sounded like a cartoon character she swiped the tears away with the back of her hand and scowled at him.

"I never claimed I wasn't," he said matter of factly. He did however open the center console and pull out a fast-food napkin that he handed to her with a grunt. "Here."

"Gee, thanks. You're such a gentleman."

He cocked up a dark brow. "You can't be all *that* upset if you can manage to be sarcastic."

"Don't you mean bitchy?" she asked.

"Your word. Not mine." He shrugged, then drew in a breath and let it out. "They really applauded?"

Of course that was what he would focus on. She let out a tearful laugh. "Yes."

"Hmm." He bobbed his head as if considering what could be a compliment in ghost-world.

"They were also wondering why an unmarried man who isn't all that old would have gotten a vasectomy."

That was a lie. She was the one wondering, not the ghosts, but he didn't need to know that.

"Who said I'm unmarried?" he asked.

Her eyes flew wide. "You're married? And we just— you know."

"Relax. I'm divorced."

"Mmm. Okay, yeah. That tracks." She nodded.

He shot her a raised brow stare before explaining, "She didn't want kids. I got snipped. Then she left me for her yoga instructor."

"Oh. Wow." Natalie cringed. "Sorry."

"Yeah, well, now you know why I'm not real fond of

people in general. And why I'm not in a relationship and have no intention of getting into one." He turned back to face the steering wheel and reached for the gear shift.

And now she knew the situation she could stop waffling about how she felt about him. He didn't date. Didn't want to. They'd had string-free amazing sex. That was all.

That should be comforting. No expectations. No disappointment. Once she let that sink in, everything would be great.

But she still didn't like him being mad at her.

"Liam?"

"Yeah?"

"It was applause-worthy sex."

His crooked smile displayed one deep dimple. "Hell yeah, it was."

Chapter Twenty-Two

Natalie heard Jules's squeal from between the bookshelves as she walked into the shop.

The girl came running to greet her at the door. "Oh my God. You're back."

Taco the tiny dog followed her, his nails clicking against the floor. Meanwhile Mr. Darcy, the snooty cat, opened one eye upon her arrival then immediately went back to napping in the sunny spot on the windowsill.

"How was it?" Jules asked.

"My trip to see my mother? Fine." Natalie pocketed the guilt about that lie to deal with later.

She was going to have to get used to these fibs if she was going to live the rest of her life denying her new ability. Or curse.

"No. Not that. I mean, yes, I'm glad your visit with

your mom was nice, but I'm talking about the road trip with the hot doctor." The words *hot doctor* were accompanied with a very suggestive wiggling of Jules's brows.

"Oh. That was fine too." Ignoring the heat she felt creeping into her cheeks, Natalie glanced around the shop.

How could it look completely different than it had just yesterday morning when she'd left it?

"You're back! How did it go?" Gabe had swooped through the front door and was in her face while she tried to juggle Jules's questions, her own lies and the fact they now apparently sold coffee mugs that read, *There might be wine in here.*

She ignored Gabe's insistent presence and tried to focus on the shop and its new inventory. "What's all this merchandise?"

Natalie moved to a shelf that had bundles of sage, lumps of what looked like amethyst, and pouches of lavender, along with the tarot cards she recognized from the night the Wiccans had met there.

"Isn't it great?" Jules asked, obviously bubbling over with excitement over the items. Meanwhile, Natalie was seeing dollar signs. The red kind since the shop had yet to operate in the black.

"How did it get here? Did you order this stuff from

somewhere?" Natalie reached out and lifted one of the dozen or so coffee mugs. This one was emblazoned with the saying, *Just give me five margaritas.*

She flipped it over to see the price on the bottom. Twenty bucks retail. Probably ten wholesale. Times twelve, unless there were more stashed somewhere. There was a hundred and twenty bucks she could add to her mounting debt.

"Nope. Red has a sublimation machine at her resale shop. She makes custom printed stuff. I told her some of my ideas and she loved them. She made all this on consignment. If it sells, she gets half the money. If not, she'll take it back. Same with the stuff from the Wiccans."

Natalie moved her attention to the tarot card display which had expanded to take up half a shelf since she'd been gone.

"Is it even selling?" she asked.

"Oh my God, yes. We sold out of the original batch of tarot cards. She had to drop off more. Oh, and she saged the shop while she was here. To ward off any evil spirits."

Glancing around, Natalie had to wonder about the effectiveness of that. Gabe was still there, but he wasn't evil so maybe sage didn't work to get rid of regular spirits.

Unaware of Natalie's new powers, Jules continued, "People are coming in asking for the new products specifically."

"How do they even know we have any of this new stuff?" she asked.

Aside from book club members, there were never more than a handful of walk-ins per day.

"TikTok! The shop's account is blowing up," Jules informed her.

"Really? Why?" Natalie was only peripherally aware the shop had a TikTok.

She hadn't created the account. She hadn't even figured out how to post on it. That was Jules and Harper's domain.

Natalie had to mute her phone when she even scrolled through it to keep the racket of the music down. It was so annoying.

"I took the 'One Margarita' sound and made it about wine and it popped off. So I immediately made another video about books. Then I made a third one about wine and books and it's going viral!"

"Hmm. I guess that makes sense, even though we don't sell the makings for margaritas," Natalie said, but she still couldn't fathom how a song about margaritas was helping them sell wine or books. Or tarot cards or coffee mugs either, for that matter.

"The romance book club wants to bring in margaritas for their next meeting, if that's all right."

"Of course. Whatever they want."

"Tonight is the mystery book club. She's bringing lemonade this time instead of iced tea."

"Good. The caffeine in the iced tea kept me awake last time."

Meanwhile, Gabe was scowling so hard at her ignoring him, she finally couldn't ignore him any longer. She turned away from Jules and toward him and mouthed, "What?"

Gabe let out a snort. "Besides the fact I'd love to know how the investigation into my *murder* went, do you know what that margarita song you're so happy is bringing people into your shop is about?"

Frowning, she pursed her lips and turned to Jules. "Um, hey, Jules. Can I hear that margarita song you're talking about?"

The most famous margarita song she could think of was by Jimmy Buffet. Not that she'd think of that song to sell wine or books. But it contained nothing to get upset about.

"Sure." Head bowed Jules scrolled through her cell then thrust her phone toward Natalie. "Here's the TikTok that's blowing up."

Assuming blowing up was a good thing, Natalie

took the cell from Jules as music blared from the device and she wondered how one tiny speaker in a cell phone could be so loud.

She turned the display to face her and watched as the singer belted out, *"Gimme one margarita imma open my legs, gimme two margaritas imma give you some head..."*

"Umm. What is this song?" Natalie asked, feeling self-conscious even holding the cell phone that emitted the profane song so loudly.

"Isn't it great?" Julia grinned.

"Gimme three margaritas imma put it in my puss, gimme four margaritas imma put it in my tush..."

As salacious as the lyrics were, what was happening on the screen might be worse. Jules danced around miming the actions described in the song with a bottle of wine and a book.

Natalie watched in horror as the bell over the store's door tinkled. Just about the time that the singer blasted out about putting it in her tush, in walked Liam.

Panicked, Natalie desperately tried to silence the song. Poking at the screen, pushing every button she could find she said, "Oh my God. How do I turn this off?"

"Gimme five margaritas mamma's havin' some fun, gimme five margaritas imma put it in your bum."

Natalie finally tossed the cell to Jules as the song

began to repeat, but it was too late. Judging by the amused and not uninterested expression on Liam's face, he'd heard it all. Even Gabe the pissed off ghost was laughing at her. But she hadn't had sex with Gabe. She had with Liam, which made this all the more embarrassing.

She stared at Liam, red-faced and appalled... and that was before she noticed Alice Mudd wiggling her ass in her own octogenarian version of the dance in the commercial fiction section.

What was it about this obscene song that made everyone crazy? She didn't know that but she did know she had to at least acknowledge Liam's presence.

Hoping her face wasn't as red as it felt, she said, "Um, hi. Can I help you?"

Dark brows cocked up over eyes the color of a stormy sea and Liam, usually king of the cranks and the smart-ass cracks, smiled wide enough his sexy as hell dimple appeared.

"For fuck's sake, Bob!" At the loud censure from a woman who didn't sound like Alice Mudd, Natalie spun back to face Jules.

She let out a little yelp when she saw the old man peering over Jules's shoulder, his hands on her hips as he watched the TikTok continue to play on a loop on her cell's screen. Meanwhile the woman who had to be his wife swatted at him.

"Get your hands off her and stop watching that!" the woman continued.

Meanwhile, Jules gave a little shiver. "Is it cold in here? The air conditioner isn't even on."

The song had even captivated the ghosts.

"Mmm. Yeah. I don't know. Old buildings, right?" Natalie turned to glare at Gabe.

"You tell me what went down in Pine Plains, I'll keep the other ghosts out of your shop. Otherwise..." He spread his palms with a shrug.

"Fine."

"Hmm?" Jules looked up after finally silencing the incessant song.

"Um, nothing. I was talking to Liam. I—uh—left something in your Jeep. Let me follow you back to the warehouse and get it." She widened her eyes hoping he'd take the hint.

He cocked one brow up. She imagined there was a silent *duh* attached. "That's why I'm here, Nat," he said in a tone laden with meaning. "Let's go."

She spun back to Jules. "Are you good here?"

Jules waived her away. "Go. I'm fine here alone."

Natalie nodded. "All right. I'll be back as soon as I

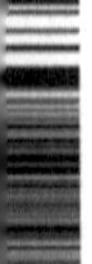

can. Um, don't make any more TikToks until I get back."

"Hey! Play that song again. I was just getting my groove on," Alice Mudd called from between the shelves.

"Sure thing, Alice." Jules smiled.

Natalie drew in a breath. She'd have to deal with all this later. First, she had her one-night stand and a murdered ghost to deal with.

"WHAT ARE YOU DOING HERE?" SHE ASKED LIAM once the shop door had closed behind them.

He snorted. "Ask your friend Gabe."

"What do you mean?"

"He wouldn't leave me alone. I guess he kept walking through me. Over and over again. He was relentless. At least I assumed it was him. It wasn't one of the old ladies, was it?" he asked, looking horrified. "They don't get some sort of *sexual satisfaction* out of that, do they?"

"Ew. No. Tell Casanova I was trying to get him to talk or get you to talk because I was tired of waiting for you to take inventory of your shop before telling me what happened."

"Why are you calling him Casanova?" Natalie asked, suspicious.

Could Gabe know what they'd done? Was there some sort of ghost gossip network? Like a game of telephone?

"Wait, what? Casanova?" Liam asked.

"Because he's cocky enough to think Ethel wants to have sex with him. By walking through him, no less. Yeah, right. Ridiculous." Gabe shook his head.

"Oh. Okay." She understood and immediately felt better.

"Natalie," Liam grit between his clenched teeth.

She sighed at his impatience. "Gabe says it's not sexual. It was him trying to get your attention. He was annoyed I was handling some business before giving him a full report of our trip."

"Oh. Okay," Liam said, echoing her.

She bobbed to the left to walk around the train worker ghost who was waiting for his train, she supposed. Meanwhile, behind them she heard once again, "Oh, for fuck's sake, Bob."

Glancing over her shoulder, she saw Bob was trailing behind her, his gaze glued to her butt. Ew. Gross.

She looked to Gabe for help.

He let out a sigh. "I'll handle it." Turning to block

the path, he said, "Come on, Bob. Leave her alone. Okay?"

Bob scowled, his wife smacked him one more time for good measure, and Natalie decided Mudville was getting a little too crowded for her taste.

"How many ghosts are in the warehouse?" she asked Gabe when he returned to walk alongside her.

"Just the two ladies. What your friend the doc does to the bodies creeps everyone else out. They tend to avoid it. Even the old guy who died in the warehouse avoids it now."

"Good." It was a sad day when a person had to take refuge with dismembered cadavers just for some peace and quiet, but she'd take what she could get.

"Enjoying your little private conversation with your buddy?" Liam asked.

"I am, yes. Thank you. Jealous?" she asked.

Liam snorted. "Yeah, right. That'll be the day."

"Um, what's this?" Gabe asked.

"What's what?" She glanced sideways at Gabe.

"This... tension." He waggled a finger between the two of them then his eyes widened. "Oh my God. You two are doing it!"

"What? No. Of course we're not." She dared to glance at Liam on the other side of her.

"He guess we had sex?" Liam asked with not an ounce of surprise in his tone.

"Why aren't you surprised?"

Liam snorted. "Maybe because you have the worst poker face in the world. You're blushing and you can barely look at me."

"He's not wrong," Gabe agreed.

She let out a huff and glared at Gabe. "Fine. Yes. We did. Once and only once. It's not going to happen again. And we are not going to speak of it ever again. If you want us to tell you what happened in Pine Plains, that's the deal." She spun to glance at Liam. "And if you want me to help you keep looking for the treasure, the same goes for you. Agreed?"

"Agreed," they said in unison both looking equally dejected.

Natalie averted her eyes to avoid seeing the mangled ghost of the guy who'd died on the train tracks. Meanwhile as Liam pulled out his key Ethel popped her head through the wall of warehouse and announced, "He's back."

Her life was truly strange and it got stranger inside as she was faced with Gabe. Not Gabe the ghost, but his body. In the flesh. And in pieces. Naked. Spread out on a table.

"Jesus, can you cover him up?" she asked, shading her eyes with her hand.

"It's no picnic for me either, sister. Bad enough he cut my head in half, but he leaves me laying around with my dick hanging out. There are ladies present, buddy! Jeez."

"Sorry." Liam pulled a piece of plastic over Gabe.

"He doesn't like you leaving him laying around naked in front of the lady ghosts. Maybe put like a towel or something over his...you know."

Liam shook his head before blowing out a breath. "This is going to take some getting used to but yeah, all right. I'll try to be more respectful of his wishes."

"Thank you," Gabe said without an ounce of gratitude in his tone.

"He says thank you," Natalie conveyed, sans bad attitude.

After an eye roll, Gabe said, "Okay, lover boy is appeased now. So talk. What happened?"

"Chill with the attitude, buddy or I won't tell you anything."

"Fine. But I bet he will." Gabe stepped around her and right through Liam.

A visible shudder ran through him. "What the hell. Why? What did I do now?"

"He wants to hear the story from you." Natalie

crossed her arms and sealed her lips. Gabe wanted to be impatient, he could just wait for her to talk.

"Fine. We met the ghost of a guy who worked at the distillery during Prohibition." Liam glanced at Natalie. "Can you at least tell me where he's standing so I know where to look?"

Scowling, she tipped her head toward where Gabe stood.

"This Charlie guy—ghost—saw you get stabbed. Said you knew the guy who did it. Your murderer called you by name. Then you said something like, 'what are you doing here?' At least that's what she told me he said." Liam hooked a thumb in Natalie's direction.

"See how easy that was?" Gabe asked, brows cocked high.

"Yeah, easy, except he left out some pretty important parts. Like how Charles says Dutch's treasure is not there. And he should know. Not only did he work there during Dutch's time, he bought the place in the sixties and owned it until he died."

"Agree to disagree." Gabe crossed his arms stubbornly.

At the same time, Liam said, "I'm not so sure Charlie would know if the treasure was there if it's well hidden."

Gabe hooked a thumb in Liam's direction. "There. See?"

Great. The only two men in her life—such as they were—were ganging up on her.

"So," she continued. "I also got in touch with your neighbor, who says she hasn't seen you."

"Duh. Because I'm dead," Gabe supplied with a good dose of cockiness.

"But now that she *realizes* she hasn't seen you lately, maybe she'll report you missing to the police and they'll make the connection with the John Doe."

"Long shot since I lived in Ohio and I died in New York, but okay."

She ignored the validity of his statement and went on. "I also tried to contact your landlord. I figured your rent must be overdue. Maybe he'll report you missing too. But he hasn't gotten back to me."

"He's a dickhead. Probably will throw my shit out on the sidewalk." Gabe scrubbed his hands over his face. "Christ. The whisky."

He looked stricken as he glanced up at Natalie.

"What's wrong?" she asked.

"I own a bottle of really rare, very valuable whisky. That son of a bitch evicts me, he'll probably drink it. Or, just as bad, toss it in the dumpster. The dumb shit won't have any idea of the value."

Natalie let out a sigh, which prompted Liam to say, "I suppose you'll tell me eventually what he's saying."

She turned to him indulgently. "He's worried about his whisky collection getting tossed when he gets evicted. It's valuable."

"He lived in Ohio, right?" Liam asked.

"Yes."

Liam whipped out his phone and Natalie began to get a bad feeling. "What are you doing?"

He glanced up at her. "It's not a very long drive."

"No." She shook her head.

"Yes! Please. You have to," Gabe begged.

"I just got back. I barely recognize my own shop after what Jules did to it while I was gone last time."

"You could sell the bottle. I don't care as long as it goes to a collector who will appreciate it. Just save it from my Neanderthal of a landlord... The bottle's estimated value is fifty-thousand dollars." Gabe let that number dangle temptingly in the air before adding, "My spare key is resting on top of the doorframe."

"Fifty-thousand dollars?" she repeated.

Liam's eyes widened. "That's how much his whisky is worth?"

She nodded then said, "Dammit."

Was it breaking and entering if the ghost of the

owner told you where the key was? She hoped they wouldn't find out.

She raised her gaze to Liam with a sigh. "When are we going?"

He grinned. "I have an intern coming in for an interview late this afternoon but tomorrow's good for me."

Interns. That was as impressive as the lab he had set up inside the warehouse that was far less impressive on the outside.

"That works for me. I have a book club coming in this evening and I'd rather not ask Jules to work a double," she told him.

He nodded. "So tomorrow then."

"Tomorrow," she agreed. She couldn't believe she agreed but she did.

Gabe cocked a brow. "I hope tomorrow's not too late."

Since a fifty-thousand-dollar bottle of booze was at risk of being guzzled by Gabe's landlord, Natalie couldn't agree more.

WIDE-EYED AS SHE WATCHED THE PARADE OF mystery book club members stream by on their way to the meeting room, Natalie leaned toward Harper. "What happened to them all?"

Each one was browner than the last, sporting a skin tone that could only be described as *leather*.

"A new spray tan place opened up. We all got coupons in the mailbox. Grand opening weekend special. All sessions were free. The old biddies can't resist a coupon."

"And they all chose the *stranded on a desert island* setting?"

"I guess they wanted to get their money's worth."

Natalie frowned. "But it was free."

"Exactly." Harper nodded.

Natalie's confusion over that logic was curtailed by the big container filled with lemonade that walked by seemingly on its own since she could barely see the tiny woman carrying it.

"Can I help you with that?" Natalie asked, stepping forward.

"I've got it, dear," Alice said from behind the container.

Natalie cringed and glanced at Harper, who shrugged.

Meanwhile, a bead of sweat dripped down Natalie's back. "Is it hot in here?"

"Yeah. A bit," Harper agreed.

"I swear the air conditioner is on." Natalie stalked to the wall unit and spread her hand in front of it only to feel heat instead of cold hitting her hand. "Crud. It's broken."

One more unforeseen expense. Wonderful.

With a pout she reached up and flipped the unit off. "I guess I'll start opening windows and prop open the door."

"Red's got a couple of portable fans for sale over in her shop. Five bucks each."

Natalie's spun to Harper. "I'll take them."

Harper smiled. "I'll see if she can run them over otherwise I'll go grab them for you."

"That would be amazing. Thank you so much."

"No problem."

Half an hour later they'd set up the fans in the windows of the shop and the meeting room. While they waited for the night air blowing in to cool the room, Harper, Red and Natalie each snuck a glass of icy lemonade.

"Mm. This is actually really good." Red pursed her lips.

"What's floating in it?" Natalie peered inside her glass.

"Lavender maybe?" Harper suggested.

Natalie took a sip. "Whatever is in here, it *is* really good." She took another long swallow and let the cold tart liquid cool her from the inside.

"Lavender. Wow. How gourmet. I didn't know Alice had it in her," Red said before taking another sip.

Harper shot her friend a sideways glance. "Be nice."

"Me? I'm always nice. And I'm also getting a refill. Anyone else?"

Another thirty minutes and two glasses of lemonade each and the three were sprawled on the carpeted kids' corner in the back of the store.

Harper leaned against one of the big balls, which rolled away and left her giggling and on her back on the floor. Natalie rested against the bookshelves feeling boneless and laughed along with her friend.

Meanwhile Red was laid flat out staring up as she said, "You should paint this ceiling back here with something cool. Like clouds. Or stars. Or ooo, some flowers."

"Flowers don't grow in the sky. But I agree with the clouds or the stars," Harper said from where she'd remained on the carpet.

Not wanting to miss out, Natalie slid down and joined the two women staring up. "I could totally paint the ceiling. I own a ladder now. So far, I might have given the hardware store as much as I gave the seller for this building."

"You should have come to me. I have a ladder for sale."

"Really? I never thought to check."

"Oh, yeah. There's nothing she doesn't have. Always check with Red first. I bought the dog's bed for in the shop at her place. And also these shoes. Aren't they cute?" Harper lifted one foot to display an adorable leopard print flat.

"Cute. And Taco has a bed in the shop now?" Natalie asked, feeling motivated as she added *paint kid's corner ceiling* to the To Do list in the Notes app on her cell while also carrying on a conversation about shopping.

"Of course Taco has a bed. I didn't want him to get jealous of the cat bed I bought at Red's shop for Mr. Darcy."

As she searched for good designs to copy on the ceiling on her cell phone, Natalie was vaguely aware of the bell above the front door tinkling but she was too busy saving an image to her camera roll to look up.

Harper, the more responsible among them apparently, lifted her head to see who was now in the front of the shop while they were laying on the floor in the back. "It's doctor hottie."

"Ugh. He probably wants to warn me to not be late tomorrow."

"And what's happening tomorrow with you and doc hottie?" Red asked.

"Nothing. We're going on another road trip."

"Oh really?" Harper asked, the question ripe with innuendo.

During the discussion she could see the top of Liam's head above the center display shelves as he looked around the shop, peeked into the meeting room, then went to stand at the bottom of the staircase. "Um, hello?"

"We're back here," Harper sing-songed.

He followed the sound of her voice and was soon standing before them, brows raised as he took in the scene of the three of them spread out on the carpet. Red still flat on her back. Harper with just her head pressed up against the ball at an awkward-looking angle and Natalie, propped up on one elbow with her cell in her hand.

"Tired?" he asked.

Natalie considered the question. "No, actually. I feel pretty good. Relaxed but focused."

Red swiveled her head on the carpet so she could say to Natalie, "Me too. That's exactly how I feel."

"And also kind of warm and fuzzy in the body. But energized in the mind," Harper explained.

"Yes!" Red and Natalie agreed at the same time.

Liam eyed the plastic cups scattered around them. "What are you ladies drinking?"

"Lemonade," Natalie answered.

"What kind of lemonade?" He reached down to pick up a cup with a bit left in the bottom and gave it a sniff.

"The tasty kind," Red answered.

"With lavender in it," Harper added.

With all the talk of lemonade, Natalie realized her mouth was dry and sat up. "I'm really thirsty."

"Me too," Red agreed.

"Let's get more lemonade," Harper suggested.

"Good idea—" Red rolled over and got on her hands and knees as she tried to stand.

"Wait. Look at me," Liam said to Natalie as she too stood, with the help of the bookshelves.

His command and the fact she actually complied with it, earned her some pretty suggestive looks from her friends. As did his gripping her chin between his thumb and forefinger as he leaned low and stared into her eyes.

"Where did you get this lemonade?" he asked.

"The old biddies," Red answered.

"Alice Mudd," Harper said at the same time.

"Old biddy Alice Mudd," Natalie summarized.

"Did she put something in here?" he asked.

"You mean besides the lavender? Like what?"

"All of your pupils are dilated. You said you're thirsty. And you're acting... weird. It's like you've been roofied or something.

Still on the floor, Harper broke out into laughter that had her kicking her feet on the carpet. "Roofied?"

"You think Alice Mudd roofied us?" Red managed to get out between gasps as she wiped the tears of laughter from her eyes.

"Can you imagine?" Natalie agreed.

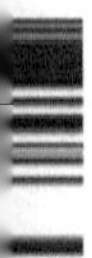

She hadn't noticed Liam leave. He just disappeared while she'd been trying to catch her breath from laughing so hard.

But he came back a minute later. Or maybe it was ten minutes later. She was having trouble with the concept of time, but eventually he was back and hawking over her with his excessive height.

"So it seems she did put something besides lavender in your lemonade. Not Rohypnol. But you all consumed a good dose of psilocybin."

"Silly what?" Red asked.

"Magic mushrooms," he explained.

Harper's eyes widened. "Ooo, what fun. I've always wanted to try shrooms."

"Alice said she only added a micro dose level to the lemonade. She said it was the same amount she added to the iced tea last time. Apparently it helps the pain in her joints so she thought everyone in the book club could benefit from it."

"Last time?" Natalie thought back, confused.

"The romance book club meeting," Harper blurted in a *eureka* moment. "Agnes asked to borrow Alice's big beverage dispenser for iced tea. Alice offered to make the tea for her and dropped it off."

Natalie's eyes widened. "I drank a bunch of that tea that night too and ended up staying awake half the night doing the rainbow bookshelf. I thought it was the caffeine keeping me up."

"I remember that." Harper nodded.

"What Alice didn't realize is that the acid in the lemon juice breaks down the psilocybin so it's absorbed more easily by the body, which didn't happen in the tea. So it can increase the effects of the same size dose dramatically."

Red held up one hand. "Hang on, professor. Chill with the science lesson for a second so we can appreciate the fact that Alice Mudd does *shrooms*."

"I know. That's weird, right? Or am I tripping?" Natalie asked.

"It was a micro dose so you're not tripping—I don't think." He frowned. "How many cups did you drink?"

"Only two," she answered.

"Actually, three," Harper corrected. "Remember? You guzzled that one then refilled it again right away."

Natalie nodded. "Right. It was so hot, I was thirsty. So three. Is that a lot?"

"It's not a little," he said.

"Well, a little or a lot, it's great. I just whipped through my entire inbox and made a kick ass list of ideas for possible future promotions for my store." Red held up her phone. "We should microdose more often."

"I agree." Harper nodded.

"First, what you consumed was quite a bit more than a typical micro dose. And then there's the fact it's currently illegal in this state."

"*Currently illegal in the state*," Natalie repeated Liam, the buzz kill, doing what she considered a pretty good, though unflattering, imitation of him. "Charlie was right. You do look and act like a G-Man."

"Yeah! You going to turn us in?" Red accused.

"I'm not going to turn you in—"

"Who's Charlie?" Harper asked over him.

The conversation was interrupted by the flood of book club members spilling out of the meeting room.

The business part of Natalie's brain took hold. She cringed. "Are they okay to drive home after being shroomed?"

"Almost all of them walked here. Mary Brimley picked up Alice in her car, but Mary wasn't drinking the lemonade. Said the acid bothers her stomach."

"Thank God for Mary's delicate stomach," Red commented.

"No kidding." Considering all the risks to her customers because of Alice drugging them, possibly without their knowledge, was harshing Natalie's mellow.

"You're going to have to speak to Alice about this for next time. You can't be dosing people and then letting them drive," Liam pointed out.

"You really are a stick in the mud." She scowled. As his brows shot up, she added, "But yes, you're right. I'll talk to her."

"Well, party's over. I'm going to go home and schedule a few newsletters with all this shroom energy." Red grabbed her empty cup off the floor.

"Yeah. Time I head out too. Stone is home waiting for me. Hmm. I wonder what sex on shrooms is like," Harper pondered.

Red laughed. "Why do I have a feeling you're going to find out?"

Natalie let out a giggle then covered her mouth after a glance from Liam.

Good nights were said then it was just Natalie and Liam, the voice of reason buzz kill.

One good thing about him being so responsible—he helped her rearrange the chairs in the meeting room and tie up the bag of trash.

Then there was nothing left to do but say good night, lock the door, turn out the lights and head to bed...

It was the saying good night part she dragged her feet on as Liam's emerald gaze held hers. "You feeling okay?"

"Great, actually."

He smiled. "Maybe I should have grabbed a cup of that lemonade for myself."

"I highly recommend it," she joked. "As long as you don't mind being a lawbreaker. Apparently, it's currently illegal in this state," she repeated that fact from his prior lecture.

"All right. I get it. I sounded like a narc. I just wanted you to be aware. You're a business owner. You don't want to incur that liability."

"Yes. Thank you for the reminder. I appreciated your shroom school." She hated when he was right but couldn't argue the truth of what he said. And he did seem to have her best interest at heart.

She hesitated, biting her lip before she raised her gaze to his again.

"That question Harper asked. About, you know, *sex on shrooms*..." She hissed the last words.

His dark brows rose. "Shockingly, that wasn't in any of the research I've read so I honestly don't know the answer."

She gnawed on her lip again before daring to raise her eyes to his. "Wanna find out?"

Her heart pounded as she watched him draw in a breath then let it out. "Is your *friend* here?"

It took her a second and then she figured out what he meant. "Gabe?"

He nodded.

She shook her head. "No. He decided the mystery book club was too boring to hang around for. He went to visit his friends in the cemetery."

His lids dropping over his eyes seductively, Liam took a step closer. "Then, yeah. I'm definitely up for a little research in that department."

Motion at the window that quickly disappeared had her thinking she might have seen Bob—as in *"For fuck's sake, Bob"*—peering through the front window.

Staunchly ignoring that possibility, she grabbed Liam's hand and tugged him in the direction of her apartment in the back. They had research to conduct.

Chapter Twenty-Five

Natalie hesitated by the door, overnight bag in her hand for the second time that week. "You're sure you are okay manning the store alone today and tomorrow until I get back?"

Looking every bit a teenager when faced with an adult questioning her, Jules rolled her eyes. "I was fine last time."

"I know. It just feels like I'm asking you for a lot lately."

"Well, you are paying me so..." Jules shrugged.

"That's true. I am." And Natalie had stopped hyperventilating over that added expense when she'd noticed the shop's sales had increased noticeably since she'd hired Jules. It didn't do much for her ego that the teen was bringing in more business than she'd been able to herself but she'd just have to get over that.

Jules's eyes widened as her gaze hit on something in front of the shop.

Natalie turned and saw Liam's Jeep pulling up to the parking spot closest to the door. She'd been hoping to get out of there early enough to intercept him at the warehouse and avoid the inevitable questions this second road trip together was going to cause with Jules.

She was about to make a quick escape before the inquisition could start, but Jules didn't ask any questions. Instead she smirked. "I see our efforts are working."

The comment stopped Natalie in her tracks.

"Wait. What? What efforts? And whose?" Natalie narrowed her eyes at the girl.

"Have you noticed anything new around the shop?" Jules asked.

A lot was new and she anticipated there'd be even more when she returned from this trip. Those were the consequences of leaving Jules unattended.

"Do you mean the new mugs?" she asked.

"No. The amethyst and lavender."

"Yes. I noticed..."

"When the Wiccans were here they placed the amethyst and lavender around to help your love life."

"And why would they do that?" Natalie asked.

"Um, Harper and I might have asked them to." Jules cringed.

"Why?" Natalie asked again.

"Because you and Liam are so perfect together," Jules began in a rush. "And you're always complaining about him but that's only because there's so much chemistry between you two—"

"So you brought in the local witches to cast a love spell?" she asked.

She was on borrowed time until Liam busted through the door and accused her of being late. But she needed answers. Not that she believed in love spells—

Although, she hadn't believed in ghosts either. *Shit.*

"Wiccans, not witches," Jules corrected. "They don't like that term. And it's not a love spell. The things they scattered around the shop are just to open you and the universe to the possibility of love."

Great. Just what she needed. The universe and the local coven throwing her at Liam who'd been very vocal about his not wanting a relationship.

It was bad enough she had trouble keeping her hands and her mind off her one-night stand as it was. Although after last night, Liam no longer qualified as a one-night stand...

Whatever he was to her, he was currently climbing out of the Jeep. Her time was up.

"Okay. I gotta go. Call if you need anything." She reached for the doorknob with one hand while grabbing her bag with the other.

"I'll be fine," Jules repeated.

"And no more love spells," Natalie hissed before she slipped through the door and slammed it closed behind her just in time to prevent Liam from trying to come inside. "Come on. Let's go."

He raised a brow and turned back toward the driver's side door. "Okay."

Again she opened her own door and stashed her own bag in the back without even an offer of help from him. Once again she reminded herself chivalry lived in romance novels, not in the hearts of modern men.

Whatever. She was a capable woman. She could open her own damn door and carry her own bag.

And she could also control her libido, even while locked inside a vehicle with Liam for hours. What had happened between them last night had been a one-time thing. The effect of Alice Mudd's magic mushrooms.

Of course, she'd assumed their treasure-hunting-slash-murder-investigation road trip had been a one-time thing too. Yet here she was sitting in the passenger seat of the Jeep heading to Ohio.

Two nights of sex. Two road trips. They were definitely *not* going to go for three of either.

A text alert seemed to blare exceptionally loudly out of her cell, earning her a quick sideways glance from Liam behind the wheel.

She looked down and read the text on the phone in her hand...and felt her cheeks heat.

HARPER

When you get back I expect a full report on all these trips you're taking with doctor hottie!

RED

And we can compare notes on shroom sex! All 3 of us I suspect.

That second text from Red, right on the heels of the first one from Harper, made Natalie realize this was a group chat, which somehow made it seem all the more embarrassing.

Natalie hit the side button to make the display go dark and pretended she wasn't appalled. She even managed to not check the phone when the alert dinged loudly one more time.

The second *ding* was harder to ignore. The third *ding*, and one more glance—or was it a glare—from Liam forced her to pick up the cell again.

HARPER

She's not going to answer. She's shy.

RED

She'll get over it.

FYI we don't believe for a second you have a wine sellers convention in the same city at the same time he has a medical conference.

Natalie smashed the button on the side with her thumb to lower the volume, then dared to look over at Liam.

"You seem to be popular today," he commented.

"Just the girls. Harper and Red. Remember? From last night," she added to remind him.

"Oh, I remember last night." There was a lilt of amusement in his tone.

She didn't know whether to attribute his smirk to his remembering her and her friends lolling on the floor high on mushrooms, or to what happened between them once they were alone.

Either way, she staunchly stared straight ahead, refusing to look at his damn dimple as it mocked her.

"We going to talk about last night?" he asked.

Her brows shot high. "You want to talk about it?"

Men weren't supposed to want to talk. And now, of

course, because last night was the last thing she wanted to discuss, he was chatty.

He raised one shoulder in a half-hearted shrug. "It was a good night."

She refused to confirm his assessment as a montage of scenes from her bedroom flashed through her head. It was like an adult film. Or maybe a modern-day Kama Sutra starring the two of them. They'd done things— She pushed that out of her mind, refusing to think more about it.

In spite of her silence, or maybe because of it, he continued, "I'm actually considering the idea of writing a paper on the effects of psilocybin on the human sex drive."

"Oh my God. Can you please stop talking?" She covered her face with her hands but peeking between her fingers saw his satisfied smile.

"God, you're so cute and adorable when you turn all red like that."

Just when she wanted to be mad at him for teasing her, he was being charming and calling her cute *and* adorable? Ugh.

"Of course there was nothing cute about you last night," he continued.

And there he was. The Liam she loved to hate. The man was infuriating.

"You were like a she-tiger," he continued. "Or a lioness. Especially when you—"

"Liam! One more word and I swear." She cut him off with a threat. What exactly that threat was, she wasn't sure, but he wasn't going to like it.

He smiled. "I'm sorry. It's just...it was a good night."

For him. All right, for her too, or it would be if she could get over the embarrassment.

She wasn't used to having porno level sex— Good porn. The classy stuff.

That's what they'd had last night. Then, while in the moment, she hadn't thought twice about it. Hadn't worried what it meant for the two of them and their lack of relationship. Now however, in the cold light of day, it was hard not to think and second guess it all, especially since he wouldn't shut up about it.

"I wonder if there's any lemonade left. I wouldn't mind trying some—"

"Liam, I swear—"

"All right. I'll stop." He concentrated on the road and was silent for a solid half a minute, then the peace and quiet ended all too soon. "I'm not joking about doing some research though."

She was willing to get out of that vehicle and walk home to end this torture. In fact, she'd just opened her mouth to tell him to pull over when he raised one hand to silence her.

"I'm not talking about the sex stuff, as intriguing as that is. But I'm serious about exploring publishing a paper on the use of psychedelics for the treatment of PTSD, and anxiety and depression. It would fall within the purview of my grant."

"You have a grant?" She twisted to stare at him.

"Yes. What do you think pays for the lab?"

"I don't know." She shrugged. "I guess I never thought about it."

In spite of how he so often proclaimed he was a doctor, she had trouble wrapping her head around him in that role. Even if he had saved her life.

Maybe it was his daily uniform of khaki pants and black logo shirt, or the muscles bulging beneath that shirt, that was throwing her off. He seemed more like a really hot EMT or something. Maybe the guy on the sidelines of the football games who runs out when someone gets hurt on the field.

She definitely hadn't pictured him getting grants, having interns and publishing papers in medical journals like a real MD or PHD or whatever.

He frowned at her. "You're a strange one."

Cute. Adorable. Lioness. And now *strange*. This conversation was going downhill rapidly.

"Well, isn't that the pot calling the kettle black," she returned.

"The old lady with the shrooms teach you that old timey saying?" He snorted.

"It's a real saying." She pouted, insulted.

"Oh, I know. I heard my grandmother say it." He smirked.

"Are you calling me old?" She glared at him.

"If it helps, you didn't remind me of my grandmother last night—"

She shot him such a scathing glare that it bought her another minute of blissful silence.

Again, that peace was broken too soon when he said, "Did you happen to pack some of those toys—"

"Liam!"

"Shutting up now."

Finally he did as he said he would and shut up... while grinning, which somehow only made her angrier than his talking had.

Chapter Twenty-Six

"HE SAID THE KEY WAS ABOVE THE DOOR ON the frame," Natalie repeated.

"I heard you the first time you said it," Liam said as he ran his fingers along the top of the door molding one more time. He turned to face her. "I'm telling you it's not there."

"So we came all this way for nothing?"

He shot her a frown. "No. Stand in front of me."

As Liam fished something out of his pocket and hunched over the knob, her eyes widened. "What are you doing?" she whispered.

"What do you think I'm doing?" he shot back.

"You're breaking in?"

"Technically, we have his permission and we would have the key if it was where he said it was. But it would be best if we didn't have to explain any of that to the cops so will you stop looking so damn guilty. Just stand still until I—got it," Liam announced as he swung the door open.

"Oh my God," she gasped.

He'd done it. Picked the lock. They were really doing this. Breaking in.

Wide-eyed she stared at him as he pocketed his lock pick set. Who traveled with lock picks? Liam did, obviously.

"Would you please get inside to have your meltdown." Liam grabbed her arm and tugged her through the doorway.

Natalie found herself inside and the door closed and locked again before she could protest.

Liam flipped on the light and they got their first glimpse into Gabe's life—from when he'd been alive.

"This place is like a museum." She skimmed her gaze over the collections. Bottles. Jugs. Photographs. Knives. Something that looked like a still. All old. All no doubt collectable.

"Or a library," Liam said as he paused in front of one of the many stacks of books that was holding down the corners of a large and very old looking map on a massive wooden table.

He picked up the receiver of a desk phone attached

by a wire and snorted. "Here's a real antique." Liam pressed it to his ear. "It's connected. There's a dial tone."

"Really? That gives me an idea." Natalie made a bee line to Liam, her cell out in one hand.

"Do tell."

"Gabe's landlord never got back to me. I left two voicemails and I emailed and no response. Don't you think that's weird? I contact him about his tenant, who's late paying his rent, and nothing. What if he's not responding because he's the killer?"

Liam's dark brows drew low. "You think? After I heard about this rare bottle of his I was thinking maybe it was one of his whisky collector buddies."

She frowned. "Who would kill someone over one fifty-thousand-dollar bottle?"

"People have killed for less. And according to Charlie, Gabe knew him and was surprised he was there in the tunnels. That fits one of his whisky buddies."

Natalie tipped her head. "It also fits the landlord and I have his phone number. We're here so I say we start with him. If it ends up being a dead end, I can ask Gabe how to get in touch with his whisky buddies."

"Fine. So what's your plan?"

"I'm going to call him from here. If he knows Gabe is dead, getting a call from his number should freak him out. Maybe enough he'll answer."

"And then what? What are you going to say if he does answer?"

"I hadn't thought that far ahead. I guess I'll say I'm Gabe's girlfriend and I came looking for him."

"His girlfriend? He's way too old for you to date."

"Well, first of all we'd be fake dating. Since, you know, he's dead. And no, he's not too old. He's a very attractive age-appropriate man."

"Oh is he?" Liam asked with attitude.

"You've only seen him dead and I agree, he probably didn't look so great. Even before you sawed his face in half." She gave a little shudder at that image while Liam rolled his eyes. "But I assure you he looks much younger alive—or as a ghost that resembles what he looked like alive, I mean. I guess. Anyway, I figure he's only in his late forties. Early fifties, max. And he kept himself very fit."

Natalie spotted a photograph on the desk amid the clutter. It was Gabe, dressed much like he was in his ghost form, on top of a mountain, smiling.

Seeing him like that—alive and happy—made her sad but she had a point to prove. "Look. He's actually quite handsome."

"Quite handsome, huh?" Liam took the framed photo she thrust at him. "So this is good old Gabe. The fit and handsome man who's probably watching you in the shower."

"Stop. He doesn't."

"Yeah, you keep believing that." Liam set down the photo and reached for the desk phone, putting his hand over the receiver as he pulled the phone farther from her. "Can I make one suggestion regarding your impending phone call?"

She let out a huff but gave in. "Sure."

"Can we get anything valuable Gabe wanted us to take out of here and stash it in a hotel room before you call the landlord and possibly bring the cops down on us?"

"So the police will have evidence that we not only broke in but also took a bunch of valuable stuff?"

"That's a very remote possibility but not at all likely. We can get a room at a hotel outside of town for the night."

"Two rooms," she corrected. She did not intend to fall any deeper into whatever this was between them.

He raised a brow. "Two rooms. But back to the situation at hand... If you call right now and the landlord comes over and kicks us out before we can grab Gabe's fifty-grand bottle of booze, this really will be a wasted trip."

"I guess either scenario is risky. Okay. We'll do it your way."

"My way," he mumbled, shaking his head. "Like this is all for *me*. Handsome Gabe's your ghost friend. Not mine."

Was he jealous? Good. His ego could stand to be taken down a notch.

She smothered a smirk of satisfaction and turned toward the back of the apartment. "He said the bottle will be in a safe in the bedroom closet. He gave me the combination."

Natalie made her way to the next room, flipping on the light there.

Liam remained back in the living room. "I guess I'd keep my booze in a safe too if it was worth that much. What else should we take? What do you think looks valuable or like something he'd want us to save? Gabe can tell you what he wants done with it when we get back to Mudville. It just seems a shame to leave it all here for the land—"

His sentence cut off mid-word, followed by a noise. Not quite a crash. More like a thud. Like something big and heavy had dropped to the carpet.

Already on her knees on the floor of Gabe's closet beneath a boggling number of hung cargo pants and long-sleeved shirts, she didn't bother getting up to investigate. But she was curious.

While squinting at the dial trying to see the numbers on the safe in the dim light, she called out, "What happened?"

He didn't answer but she was too busy trying to figure out how to shine her cell phone flashlight at the safe. She needed one hand to hold all of Gabe's clothes out of the way so she could see and the other hand to spin the dial.

There was another crash just as she tried securing the phone in her bra. "Don't be dropping his stuff. You're going to have to explain to Gabe yourself if you break something."

When there was still no answer, and she still couldn't see the numbers clearly enough to open the safe because the cell kept falling out of her bra, Natalie gave up and stood.

Of course Gabe couldn't have a simple safe with a nice lit digital keyboard. She shouldn't be surprised since he still owned a landline...the kind with a cord.

She'd have to have Liam hold her cell phone for her so the flashlight lit the dial while she entered the long and complicated combination consisting of lefts and rights and multiple turns for each number.

First she'd have to find him.

Maybe he'd taken a load of stuff out to the Jeep.

Natalie emerged from the bedroom and stopped dead in her tracks.

She was vaguely aware of a scream. It took her a second to realize it was her own. Though she wasn't sure which she'd screamed about. Because of Liam's lifeless body on the carpet, blood pooling beneath his head as a man stood over him with the bronze urn he'd hit him with, or because of the second man who jumped out of the shadows to strangle the first man.

Chapter
Twenty-Seven

THINGS HAPPENED FAST—AT THE SPEED OF light. A jumble of events that swirled in her mind. It didn't matter in what exact order it all happened. The end result was the same. And that was Natalie, sprawled on the floor with her hands zip-tied behind her back.

Next to her sat Liam, also bound behind the back. Also on the floor. Still bleeding but still breathing and thankfully conscious though groggy.

As they were she couldn't even help him, nor could he help himself.

"Do you want to lay your head in my lap? Maybe the pressure will stop the bleeding," she offered, feeling helpless.

"Thank you, but it'll be fine."

She wasn't so sure about that.

"Aw. How sweet." That sarcastic comment came from the man on the other side of Liam. The one who'd caused the head wound in the first place.

The only person missing was the assailant. He'd rendered the man who'd hit Liam unconscious, which at first had given her hope. That was until he came after Natalie. After a brief chase around Gabe's desk he finally caught her.

He'd tied her up first, then the two unconscious men, then he'd left. She could only hope for good.

Now that Liam was awake, they could plan how to get out of there.

But first...this seemed like a good opportunity to get acquainted with the asshole who'd knocked out Liam.

"And who are you?" she asked, leaning forward to be able to see the man past Liam.

"I could ask you the same thing since I own this place and you're trespassing."

This was Gabe's landlord? The man she'd been so sure was the killer, though that was looking less likely since he was in the same predicament as the two of them. Although he had hit Liam. And who was the other guy? Was he the real killer?

So many questions flooded her thoughts, all of which were interrupted by Liam's snort.

"Told you it wasn't the landlord," Liam mumbled.

"Who then?" she asked.

"Why not the whisky collectors? Is it so hard to believe I'm right for once?" he countered in spite of his blood loss.

Frustrated enough without Liam being annoying, besides the fact they might be murdered at any moment, Natalie leaned forward to be able to see the landlord again.

If she was going to die, she'd do it having answers.

"Why did you sneak into the apartment and hit Liam over the head?"

"First, I thought you were robbing the place. That's what made me come over to begin with. I saw the Jeep and the lights on inside. But then I heard you talking about bringing all this stuff to Gabe, so I figured he'd sent you to grab his shit so he could skip out on the rent."

"That's still no reason to hit someone." She scowled. "And why didn't you call me back. If you are so worried about getting the rent payment, you'd think when a person calls and emails saying they might have information about your missing tenant you'd respond."

He huffed out a breath. "I guess it doesn't matter now so I might as well tell you. I wanted that fancy old sword of his. The one hanging on the wall. I figured if he wasn't coming back I'd run out the clock, legally evict him and take whatever I wanted."

"That's pretty shitty."

He shrugged. "What can I say?"

"See. He's a shithead but he's not Gabe's killer," Liam pointed out.

The man's eyes widened. "Whoa. Wait. What now? Gabe's dead?"

"Yup." Liam nodded then said with a wince, "Ow. My head."

"Hey, but wait a minute. What's going on here? You two were talking about bringing all this stuff to him. He ain't really dead. You're lying."

"Oh, I assure you, he is. Very dead. This guy here has got Gabe's dismembered body stashed in his warehouse."

The landlord drew back. He even scootched backward a bit, farther away from Liam before he asked, "So *you* killed him."

"No, I didn't kill him. I got him already dead." Liam's cryptic denial didn't seem to pacify the landlord.

"I still don't get it. You said you were going to ask Gabe what to do with his stuff when you got back. I heard you."

"Long story," Liam said at the same time Natalie said, "Gabe Senior."

She shot Liam a glare before she continued.

"Gabe's father. Same name," Natalie supplied on the fly, proud of herself for such a smooth lie. She was getting good at this. Maybe there was hope for her yet.

Liam let out a breath. "Yeah. What she said."

"He never said anything to me about a father."

"Well, you two weren't exactly buddies now were you? You were going to evict him and steal his stuff," Natalie pointed out.

The landlord didn't deny the truth, but he did make a face.

Natalie wasn't done with him yet. "Can you think of anyone who'd want to kill him?"

"No. We weren't exactly buddies, remember?" After a pause, he asked, "How'd he bite the dust, anyway?"

"Stabbed in the back with a knife."

"Yeesh. That's a hell of a way to go. Guns give a certain amount of distance. Poison is even more detached. But stabbing. That's up close and personal. That could be a clue to your killer, right there."

The man had obviously considered various methods of murder in disturbing depth, but he had a point.

If the motive was personal, emotional, it could have stemmed from professional jealousy or competition.

She turned to look at Liam. "Maybe it *is* another collector."

"Thank you. Finally," Liam said, shooting her a glare while wiggling around on the floor. Come to think of it, he'd been wiggling around for a while.

"What's wrong with you? Do you have to pee?" she asked. If so, that was going to be awkward.

"Shhh."

She was about to yell at him for shushing her when the door opened…

Chapter Twenty-Eight

The landlord's eyes widened at his first sight of the man standing in the doorway. The same man who'd choked him out from behind. "You!"

"You know him?" Natalie asked.

"Sure do. He's been squatting at his girlfriend's place right next door for going on six months now."

The landlord knew the possible killer. He was dating the woman next door. Margot. Natalie had messaged with Margot about Gabe when they'd been in Pine Plains. Margot had been hesitant to report Gabe missing.

The pieces of the puzzle began to fall into place and the picture they formed was not good.

"You killed Gabe," she blurted, raising her gaze to the tall, shaggy-haired man standing over them.

"Yup. The little pissant." The man picked the sword off the wall to inspect it more closely.

He hadn't covered his face. They could identify him. He'd admitted being a murderer.

She'd seen enough crime shows to know he wasn't planning on letting them go.

"You can't kill us. You'll get caught," she said.

Shooting her a glance, he said, "Haven't gotten caught yet."

"People know we're here." Not at all true, but she hoped he bought the lie.

But why oh why hadn't she just told her friends the truth? About all of it. Gabe and the other ghosts. Her and Liam.

This guy could murder them all and dump their bodies just like he had Gabe's and no one would ever know. She'd just disappear. Harper and Jules wouldn't even know where to start looking for her.

And—oh God—they were so far from home they might end up as John Does too. Then the coroner would donate their bodies to science and some cadaver lab like Liam's would be sawing her head in half too.

Black started to appear on the edges of her vision. Dizzy, she was grateful she was already on the floor. She let her head drop between her knees to keep from passing out. She wanted to be conscious for what little time she had left. Aware right up to the end of her short life.

Of course, she might change her mind about that depending on what method he planned to use to murder them.

With her head still buried between her knees, she didn't see but she heard it—quick, sudden motion right next to her. She raised her head in time to see the scuffle between Liam, now on his feet with his hands somehow free, and the killer.

It was like she and the landlord were the audience for a prize match, but this was by no means an equally matched fight.

Or maybe it was more like she was watching a movie because there was a clear hero and an obvious villain in this match-up. She hoped that, like all good movies with a satisfying ending, the good guy would win.

It certainly looked like he would. Liam was like a beast in his intensity. Like a ninja in his precision.

She'd always had trouble picturing him as a doctor, but she had no problem now picturing him as a trained military fighter. He'd snapped back into fighting mode —warrior mode—like the years since he'd been out of the service and in the medical field didn't exist.

A sweep of a leg. The smooth grasp and twist of an arm. A headlock. The smashing of a body against the floor. In four moves, a beautiful choreography, Liam had the killer pinned, his face ground into the carpet, his arms behind his back.

He'd never been more attractive. He'd totally redeemed himself for not opening the car door or helping her with her luggage.

Who needed a guy who opened doors when she had a warrior?

He'd saved her life. He'd taken out a killer with his bare hands.

He was a bad ass—who also had quite a fine ass. Liam was both beautiful and deadly and she was in danger of falling madly in love with him at that moment, which would be the dumbest thing she could do considering his anti-relationship proclamation.

She was definitely madly in lust with him.

If they were alone and he wasn't currently sitting on top of a murderer—and if the shithead landlord wasn't there—she'd have jumped him already.

Had he gotten better looking? She stared at him deciding if she was in some sort of shock induced rapture or if he'd actually gotten more handsome in the past day.

"Hey! Nat. Snap out of it. I need you to get on that damn ancient landline and call nine-one-one. Then bring me the phone cord so I can tie him up until the police get here."

He might be more handsome but he was still as bossy as ever, but it didn't piss her off as much as usual.

Still, what he was asking her to do was impossible.

"My hands are literally tied. Behind my back." She widened her eyes at him in a *what do you expect me to do* expression.

"Use your nose to dial," he suggested as this surreal situation took a turn for the ridiculous.

Past being proud, she didn't have much choice but to try it. She certainly wasn't going to risk the bad guy getting away from Liam by asking him to make the call himself or cut her ties.

She struggled to her feet and walked to the phone on the desk.

Even more amazing than her willingly taking orders from Liam was that the nose dialing worked. Thank goodness Gabe had at least upgraded his landline to a push button from a rotary phone at some point.

She even managed to unplug the phone from the wall behind her back and carry the whole thing over to Liam.

He made short work of tying up the bad guy's hands and feet, after which he made the landlord sit on him—just in case the murderer got a surge of adrenaline and tried to escape—while he cut the zip-ties off both of their hands.

Then all they had to do was wait for the police to arrive.

Although, while they had the time.

"Why did you kill Gabe?" she asked him.

"None of your fucking business."

"Was it over the treasure?"

"Treasure?" the landlord asked, perking up.

"Yeah, it was over the fucking treasure. What do you think? That guy Gabe was always bragging to my girl about all his clues and maps and historical knowledge and shit. And how rich he was going to be after he found that gold and diamonds from that mobster. So I followed him."

"And stabbed him with his own antique knife," Natalie guessed.

"Yeah. So what? He died doing what he loved. Isn't that the dream?" The guy snorted.

"Did your girlfriend know?" she asked, feeling betrayed.

Natalie had messaged the woman. She'd seemed genuinely concerned about him.

"No. I was gonna surprise her with it when I found it first. So then she'd stop fawning all over him. *He's so smart. He knows so much.* Ugh."

"So you stabbed him because you were jealous?"

"No, I stabbed him because he shot off his smart

mouth. Said Margot could do better. And maybe he'd ask her out when he got back. I guess I lost my temper."

Liam sucked in air between his teeth and shook his head. "Oh, Gabe."

"That's insane. Who could do that? Kill someone over something so minor."

"Don't try to make sense out of the senseless, Nat. You can't," Liam said.

"I mean, I can kind of understand. The guy did have a smart mouth on him sometimes." The landlord held up his hands palms out when Natalie whipped her gaze to him. "I'm not saying that's grounds for murder..."

As Natalie tried to figure out how they could press charges for assault against the landlord even though they'd technically broken in themselves, she heard the sound of sirens.

Chapter Twenty-Nine

THE GOOD NEWS WAS THAT NATALIE'S LYING skills were on point.

Thanks to her fast talking she and Liam were not going to be charged with breaking and entering.

The bad news was, it seemed neither was the landlord going to be charged with his assault on Liam since he was the property owner and he claimed he thought they were intruders.

While the EMTs stitched up Liam's head wound, she told the police they'd used the spare key they knew Gabe kept above the doorframe to get in. They'd come to check on him because, as his longtime friends, they knew where the key was and were concerned about him after an uncharacteristic and prolonged lack of communication.

"Where is this key?" the officer asked.

Liam's gaze cut to her from beneath the gauze the EMT used to clean his head.

"I, uh, left it on the desk when we first got here. Is it not there?" she asked, smoothly.

A second officer moved to the desk. "Not seeing it."

"The bad guy must have taken it after he tied us up. He disappeared and left us alone for a while."

The officer nodded, jotting everything down in his little notebook without question.

A surge of pride swelled inside her. Later, after she was home and life was normal—or as normal as it could get given she now saw ghosts—she'd have to evaluate how she probably shouldn't feel so accomplished about being an expert liar.

For now, the deception was necessary and for a good cause. And thanks to her believable story, her police interview went smoothly. Right up until the officer flipped his notebook shut and told her she could go.

"Um, can I ask what's going to happen to the guy who tied us up?" she asked.

"Because of the nature of Mr. Walsh's injuries sustained during the fight, the assailant will probably be charged with one count of felony assault and three counts of unlawful imprisonment."

"But he admitted to all three of us that he killed Gabe Miller."

"Without a body or a murder weapon or evidence of any kind we can't charge him with murder. I'm sorry." The officer turned to go and Natalie panicked.

"Wait! Um, the last time I heard from Gabe he'd been heading to Pine Plains, New York. That was months ago and I haven't heard from him since. That's why I was so worried. Is there any way you could maybe check with the Pine Plains police? What if the police there found Gabe's body but couldn't identify him? Wouldn't he just be a John Doe then?" Since theoretically she shouldn't know for sure that Gabe was dead, she added, "Of course, I hate to even think that because I really hope Gabe is fine, but could you check?"

The officer looked skeptical, but finally nodded. "All right. I'll make a call."

"Thank you so much."

With their statements given and them both in the clear, they were dismissed. While police car lights continued to flash and one officer stretched crime scene tape across Gabe's doorway, she and Liam walked to the Jeep in the parking lot and just sat there, in the dark, silent.

Liam broke the silence first. "Good job about Pine Plains."

"Thanks. Sorry about us not being able to get the booze out and that this was a wasted trip."

He turned to her and shook his head. "Not wasted. We solved Gabe's murder. That's more important. Maybe now he'll be able to move on."

"You think?"

"Maybe. You're the ghost expert." As Liam started the engine, Natalie felt a little bit of panic mixed with sadness at the thought.

What if Gabe's spirit did move on?

She might complain about him but, strange as it seemed, she'd miss him being around.

They drove in silence to the nearest hotel, though truth be told she probably should have driven since Liam was concussed. She had offered but apparently doctors made really bad patients.

At the hotel, he cut the engine and glanced at her. "You can wait here if you want. I'll go in."

"Please let me pay this time—"

"Nope." He reached for the driver's side door handle.

"Liam."

Stepping down, he glanced back. "Yeah?"

"Get only one room. I—after all that's happened, I don't think I want to be alone." That was completely true.

He nodded, slammed the door closed and headed toward the office.

She was still shaken, but what she didn't also mention was that Liam, in his condition, shouldn't be alone.

Then there was that third reason she didn't even want to admit to herself—her renewed desire for him. After his hero act, that craving for him had hit her extra hard tonight. As bad as when she'd been under the influence of Alice's mushrooms.

However they did not have sex after checking in to the single room with only one big bed.

Between Liam's concussion and her distress, even with his heroics getting her all worked up, she'd been happy to just fall asleep with him in the bed next to her while knowing the killer was in custody.

The morning, however, was a different story. Once again she awoke with Liam's morning wood poking her in the backside as he spooned her.

She rolled over to face him and watched as he slept. Creepy and stalkerish, maybe. But their ad hoc partnership was over. There wouldn't be any more road trips to look for treasure or the killer.

They weren't dating. She wasn't even sure they were friends. And she didn't want to be a hook-up. A booty call. Given that, this might be the last time they ever shared a bed. And if this did turn out to be the final time she ever woke next to him, she figured she should try to remember every last detail.

His eyes fluttered open and she was caught staring. She tried to cover for the weirdness with, "Good morning. How do you feel?"

She knew one part of him was feeling fine, but she didn't mention that.

"I'll live," he said. Then rolled over and stood, saying to her over his shoulder on the way to the bathroom, "Will you be ready to hit the road soon?"

Yes, she'd vowed to herself it would only be a two-night stand. Yes, she'd initially told him yesterday to get two rooms. So why then did his nonchalance hurt so bad?

Maybe because the hottest man she'd ever been with had just walked away from her in spite of his raging hard-on. The disappointment settled deep inside where she had a feeling it would reside for a good long while.

"Uh. Yeah. For sure. I'll be ready," she answered.

After a nod, he locked himself in the bathroom. She actually heard the lock.

As she decided what she felt about that, her phone rang and an unknown number appeared on the display. She answered it.

Already assaulted with mixed feelings, it was just the

icing on the crappy cake to hear the police officer's voice telling her he had bad news. An unidentified male matching Gabe's description had been found dead in Pine Plains and declared a John Doe.

For Gabe—and for her too—this should have been good news.

Somehow she didn't feel good.

Chapter Thirty

With the win of solving Gabe's murder tempered by the loss of the fifty-thousand-dollar bottle and the possible loss of ghost Gabe in Natalie's life, in addition to the obvious end of her sexual relationship with Liam, the mood in the Jeep was pretty dreary as Liam pulled up to the front of her shop in Mudville.

"Thank you for driving," she said, resorting to niceties for lack of anything else to say.

"Thank you for letting me be part of your adventures."

The adventures which were now over.

Hating that thought, she grasped at an excuse to stay in touch. "It's been so crazy, I forgot I promised to ask Gabe about the cause of his head injuries. And anything else about his medical history that might help you. I'll do that right away and I guess email you?"

"Thanks. That would be a big help." He reached for the compartment in the console and pulled out a business card. "My email address is on there."

A business card. He couldn't have given her a clearer sign that whatever they'd had was over. She forced a smile anyway.

"Great. Thanks." Overnight bag in her lap, she reached for the door handle. "So I'll see you around."

He dipped his head. "See you."

After that, she couldn't get out of the Jeep fast enough.

Getting dumped was bad. Getting ghosted also bad. But this interaction felt almost like it was both. There had been no dumping. No ghosting, but his taking a huge step back and acting as if they hadn't even been together was weird. And hurtful. And probably exactly what she should have expected from him.

She walked through the front entrance to find the store packed. That should have been a good thing. But today all she wanted to do was curl up alone with a pint of ice cream and the television remote.

Since that obviously wasn't going to happen until at least six tonight, if not later if there was a meeting, she pasted on another fake smile and moved toward the check-out counter.

"Do you see this crowd?" Jules, ever bubbly, asked.

Stashing her overnight bag under the counter, she said, "I do. What's going on?"

Had Jules autonomously run a fifty percent off sale or something? It was probably for the best there'd be no more road trips with Liam. She needed to take care of her business. Why did she think she could leave her livelihood in the hands of an eighteen-year-old?

"We're having Tarot readings in the meeting room today. Look how many people it attracted."

"I see. Are they buying anything or just getting a reading?"

"Oh, they're buying. We've had more sales than any other day since I've worked here and there's hours left until closing."

Natalie noticed the people in the store did look like they were shopping. Most had a book or a bottle of wine in their hand. One coming toward the register now had two coffee mugs plus a tote bag.

When had they started selling tote bags? She was afraid to ask.

Leaving Jules to check out the customer she'd already greeted and begun to ring up, Natalie moved toward the meeting room where there seemed to be a line formed that extended through the door and into the shop.

"You're back!" Harper greeted. "Isn't this turnout amazing?"

"It sure is. How did this all come about?" She'd only been gone since yesterday morning.

"One of the Wiccans came in yesterday and we all got to talking about Tarot and before I knew it she'd offered to do free readings. I put the idea out on social asking if anyone would be interested and we had so many responses we decided to do it right away. We've sold two dozen sets of tarot cards already just today. Plus the sage and amethyst is moving too."

"Wow." Natalie took in the scene. There'd never been this many people in the shop ever. Not even on book club nights. She should be thrilled.

Why wasn't she thrilled?

"Is this okay that we did this? I'm sorry. I should have called you first. I honestly figured we'd get a handful of people all day—"

"No. Harper it's fine. This is amazing."

"You just don't look very happy." Harper's eyes widened. "Oh. Did something happen between you and Liam?"

The question inexplicably had tears stinging behind her eyes. "What could have happened? We're not dating or anything. Just was a long couple of days on the road. That's all." That lie—in spite of her newfound claim of expertise in that area—came out sounding flat.

"Okay." Harper nodded. "But if you ever want to talk—"

Natalie nodded. "I have your number and I know where to get the best margaritas."

"Yes you do." Harper smiled. "Hey. Do you want to go decompress for a bit? Eat or grab coffee or a shower or whatever? Jules and I can handle the shop."

She couldn't keep dumping her responsibilities on Jules, who was supposed to be a part time helper, and Harper, who she didn't pay at all. But there was one thing she wanted to do.

"Actually, yeah. Just give me a few minutes, then I'll be back."

"Take all the time you need. We're good."

Natalie made her way back through the shop, looking but not finding what she sought.

Not only was Gabe not visible, but she didn't see any ghosts. Not one.

Was Liam right? Was the whole ghost thing somehow connected to Gabe's murder and now that was solved her powers had disappeared along with Gabe's ghost?

Starting to panic, she reached past Jules, grabbed her

bag as an excuse and said, "I'm just going to drop this in my apartment then be back."

"Take your time. I'm good," Jules said echoing Harper's sentiment and making Natalie wonder if she really wasn't needed around there at all.

That was a concern for later. Right now, she needed answers of a more ethereal kind.

He wasn't in the shop. He wasn't in her apartment. She peered out the window toward the warehouse but saw nothing but Liam's Jeep. Surely, if Gabe was inside the lab he would have seen Liam's return, known she was home too and been over here.

She didn't see the mangled man on the tracks. Nor did she see the guy going to work on the railroad. Even For Fuck's Sake, Bob and his wife were missing.

Hidden away in the back corner of the store—the local history section—the tears threatened again. Was she really going to cry over the loss of a gift she'd never wanted? The one she'd never appreciated until it was gone.

"Hey, you're back."

She spun away from the window and let out a sob when she saw him.

He was the best sight she'd seen all day—Indiana Jones hat, cargo pants, vest and all.

"Gabe." She realized she was in public and glanced

around to make sure no customers had heard. "Follow me."

She led the way back to her apartment then collapsed against the door after she closed them inside. "You're still here."

"Where else would I be?" he asked, looking confused.

She drew in and let out a breath to calm herself before she answered. "I thought you might have moved on."

"Moved on? Like to... heaven?" He frowned.

"Yes. Or wherever ghosts go when they don't stay here. Do you know where they go?"

"No, I don't. And why would you think I'd moved on?"

The dark cloud of worry seemed to lift from her soul as she said, "The man who killed you is in police custody and the Pine Plains police have identified your body. You're no longer a John Doe."

"And? Who was it?"

"Your neighbor's boyfriend. He was jealous."

Gabe shook his head. "Mother fucker. I never would have guessed him."

"I know, right? Me either. I had it pinned on the landlord, who is an ass, by the way. Liam thought it was one of your whisky collector buddies."

"The whisky." His eyes widened with the memory. "Did you—"

She shook her head. "No. The police showed up before I could get it out of the safe. Then your apartment was a crime scene and Liam wanted to head home—"

"Crime scene?"

"I guess I have a lot to tell you."

"You think?" he asked, his sarcastic eye roll not even annoying her today.

She might not have Liam in her life but at least she still had Gabe.

Chapter Thirty-One

"Natalie, you have to have a reading," Jules insisted at the end of the day when the line of patrons waiting had finally dissipated.

She shook her head. "No—"

"Why not?"

"She's been working hard all day at this. I'm not going to make her—"

"Come." The Wiccan, dressed more like a hippy than a fortune teller, summoned Natalie with the crook of one finger.

"I really don't—"

"Do not be afraid," she said with a slight but surreally on point accent Natalie couldn't quite place.

"I'm not afraid."

"Oh, but you are," she said, with the slightest bow of her gray head.

Insulted at being called both a chicken and a liar in the span of two sentences by a woman she didn't even know, Natalie said, "Fine."

She stalked to the chair and sat, taking the deck of cards from the woman who, with the flip of her waist-length hair said, "We will do a three-card draw. Past, present and future. Nothing to be nervous about."

"I'm not nervous," Natalie protested, even though she might be a little nervous.

"Please, cut the cards," she requested.

Natalie did, after which the woman took back the deck and proceeded to lay out three cards.

"We'll start with the past." She flipped the first card over. "The Magician. A positive card which could mean in your past you've been empowered to make something happen."

Damn. Natalie had done that. She'd left her job and opened this shop. Although she didn't tell the Wiccan that, she did nod.

"Representing your present is... the Death card." The Wiccan raised her gaze to meet Natalie's. "Do not be concerned. The Death card can mean many things. An ending. A transformation or the start of a new phase in your life, for instance."

Natalie let out a laugh. "I'm actually not too worried about that one."

There had indeed been an ending in her life—her sex life. And given the fact she could now see the dead the card seemed pretty spot on.

Although, the accuracy of the cards was starting to creep her out a bit. Enough she wasn't sure she wanted to see the future card.

The Wiccan nodded and reached for the last card. "The future card is the Lovers. Possibly meaning the finding of a soulmate or kindred spirit."

Natalie let out a low groan,

The Wiccan's eyes came up. "Or, in your career, a new mutually beneficial business association perhaps."

Happier with that interpretation, Natalie said, "Thank you. That was...more fun than I expected."

"My pleasure." The woman began gathering her cards, finally done after what had been a long day.

It was six. Jules had locked the door and flipped over the *Closed* sign. And last she'd checked the receipts, it had been a stellar day for sales.

"Please, let me pay you something for your time," Natalie offered as a wave of guilt hit her.

"No need."

"I'd really like to do something for you. Can I send you home with some wine or a book?"

The woman tipped her head slightly to the side and evaluated Natalie for an uncomfortably long time. "You can do something. But for you. Not for me."

"All right..." Natalie said to break the silence that stretched out between them.

"Embrace your gift." With that, the woman stood, cards in hand, and headed toward the doorway leaving Natalie with her mouth open and no words.

"I think you should listen to her."

She spun to see Gabe. As much as she was glad he was the only one in the room to hear that cryptic advice, she was still unwilling to answer him while Jules and Harper were just through the doorway in the shop. She rolled her eyes at him and headed to the shop.

He, of course, followed her, still talking. "And I don't mean about your gift—although that was pretty creepy how she knew, huh. I mean about that Lovers card."

She turned to shoot him a silent frown.

"Your doctor is over there chopping the hell out of poor Ethel's body. And he's got some really annoying music blasting loud enough to wake the dead—pardon the expression. I don't know what happened between you two but it's got him hella agitated."

She didn't want to think about Liam and she refused to believe that if he was agitated it had anything to do with her. She was fine believing the Lovers represented Harper and Jules and the success of the shop thanks to their collaboration. She certainly didn't need Gabe putting any ideas in her head about Liam.

That chapter of her life had ended, as evidenced by that Death card.

"Hey, how about margaritas at the Muddy River Inn to celebrate today's success?" she asked Harper and Jules. "On me. But yours, Jules, has to be non-alcoholic."

Jules's, "Aww. Can't I have just one?" was buried under Harper's enthusiastic, "Yes! Sounds good to me."

With a glance back at Gabe, Natalie grabbed her keys, phone and wallet and closed the door on him and any hope of romance. Success was far more satisfying and lasted longer than sex anyway.

It turned out Gabe wasn't quite that easy to ditch. Apparently he could go to the bar. He even sidled up to a couple of ghosts inside and had a good old time for himself.

That was one reason she cut the night short after two rounds and a platter of wings for the table. The other reason was she didn't want Jules's parents mad at her for keeping her out late at the local dive.

Besides, she was exhausted. But there was still one thing she wanted to do tonight.

When Harper had left with Jules—she was dropping

her home—Natalie turned to Gabe, who was conveniently next to her in the parking lot.

"You have plans for tonight?" she asked.

He shot her a glare. "Yeah, I thought I'd hit up Tinder and find myself a date."

"No need to get nasty. I meant I know you like to go to the cemetery."

"I don't particularly *like* to go to the cemetery. There's just not much else to do when you're dead. Why?"

"I was hoping you could help me out with something."

There was one piece of unfinished business left.

If she was going to move on she needed to close the book on that chapter completely. That meant keeping her promise to one Doctor William Walsh, Director, The Human Institute... at least that's what his business card said.

Chapter Thirty-Two

THE SHOP WAS BLISSFULLY SILENT THE NEXT morning as Natalie flipped the *Closed* sign to *Open* and unlocked the door.

The cat was there and ignoring her, as usual, but the dog came and went with Jules and she'd given her the day off.

The girl had worked more than her share of hours recently. Besides that, Natalie could use some time alone in the store to get her bearings again after all the changes —both in her life and in the shop.

Her peace and quiet was short lived.

She had just hit the switch to turn on the meeting room lights so she could straighten up after the prior day's Tarot Fest when she heard the bell above the front door.

With a sigh she headed back to the shop portion of the building and stopped.

"Liam."

"Nat."

Well, that was a real promising start to a conversation —*not*.

"I, uh, wanted to say thank you. For the medical history you sent me for Gabe. I can't tell you how valuable that information is. We don't get a whole lot of personal information with the cadavers. To maintain their privacy. But having all the details will really help in my research."

Okay. This could be nice. Liam, polite and grateful. A casual conversation about his job.

Maybe they *could* survive as neighbors in a post hook-up world.

In spite of the residual shadow of disappointment over this new normal, she forced a small smile. "Of course. I was happy to help. Um, you know, if you wanted me to, I could interview the other cadavers' ghosts for you."

"Really? That would be amazing. Thank you."

"You're welcome."

Now this was just getting weird. Where was snarky Liam, the smart-ass doctor she loved to hate? She missed their playful banter. His snipes and her clever retorts.

This was just boring. She wanted fire and... and... fireworks. What she had before with Liam. Because if she couldn't have love, she'd take him as a frenemy.

It would be better than this... him as a cold casual acquaintance or even as a polite but lukewarm friend.

Meanwhile, he was still there. Silent, but his eyes darted from the floor to the ceiling to the cat then back to her.

"Was there anything else?" she asked.

He hesitated, drawing in a breath that had his beautiful chest rising beneath the ever-present black shirt before he blew it out.

"Natalie," he finally began again. "I've fought—and lost the battle—against what I feel. Unwelcome as these feelings are, I can't suppress them anymore. I have to tell you how much I like you... More than like you. Much more."

As a book nerd, Natalie had reread Jane Austen's *Pride and Prejudice* annually since college. As a romance lover and a television addict she'd watched, more than once, every iteration of the movies based on the book.

But even if she had been just a casual reader of the work she would have recognized the similarities between Liam's reluctant profession of love and Mr. Darcy's.

It was that speech which, in the original work, insulted Elizabeth Bennett so badly that she spews at him an insult-filled monologue of her own, seemingly irrevocably casting him out of her life forever, in spite of his extreme hotness and even more extreme wealth.

It was as if Natalie was still sleeping and deep in a dream where her subconscious had taken the characters and settings of her own life and inserted them into Austen's most famous plot.

Maybe she was still in her bed, in which case she figured she might as well do what she wanted.

She took two rapid steps forward. "You really are just like Mr. Darcy. Lucky for you I'm nothing like Elizabeth Bennett."

When she reached him, she threw her arms around his neck, rose on tiptoe and crashed her mouth against his.

She kissed him like it was the last time, or maybe the first time. Without regard to their strange though brief history together. In spite of his rather uncomplimentary profession of his feelings.

In case it wasn't already obvious by the way she was sucking on his face, she pulled back from the kiss far enough to say, "Just so you know, I've caught feelings for you too. And I hate it. But I'm done fighting, as well."

A wave of relief, maybe even happiness, washed over his expression but he didn't have time to respond before her mouth covered his again and her tongue met his.

She pressed her lower half against him. She wanted to make sure he knew this chapter was going to end up in her bed.

The bell tinkled again and Natalie realized not only was the shop officially open to customers, but she and Liam were also making out while blocking the front door.

"Get a room, you two."

Natalie took one step back and could see Alice Mudd, heads shorter than Liam, motor her short little legs around them as she headed toward the aisle not with the women's fiction, not with the cozy mysteries, but the one with the Wicca merchandise.

Her shop was changing this town and the people in it. Which was only fair since she was pretty sure this town had changed her. And Liam.

She raised her gaze to meet his.

He brought his hands to her shoulders and asked, "So what now?"

"I guess maybe we should go on a date?"

They'd already gone treasure hunting, investigated a murder, been taken hostage and had sex. But technically they'd never been on a date.

"So you mean like dinner at the Mudville House and a movie at the Drive-In?" he asked with a smirk.

Not just because their options were very limited here

in Mudville, but also because that sounded absolutely, wonderfully normal, she said, "Perfect."

He nodded. "It's a date."

Then, just when she thought—feared—that compliant, polite Liam might be the new normal, he glanced toward the back of the shop.

"Hey, Alice. Do you think you could make us some of that special lemonade of yours?"

"Sure thing, Doc," she said with a salute.

As Natalie's eyes widened in shock, he grinned down at her. "We have to do *something* after the movie."

She let out a breathy laugh as her pulse sped at the thought. "Yeah, we do."

The hot but cocky doc she'd fallen in love with was back and she couldn't be happier.

Epilogue

SIX MONTHS LATER

"Maybe I shouldn't go. We might get busy." Natalie stood by the door, second guessing this trip for so many reasons.

Jules let out a breath. "Nat, it's only for three days. Black Friday is over and Christmas isn't for weeks yet. I doubt we're going to get mobbed."

"But we just got that delivery of Beaujolais Nouveau—"

"If we get a sudden run of people needing wine I'll call Harper to help me. I promise."

"You're sure you don't have to miss any of your college classes to work—"

"I'm sure...and your ride is here. Go. Visit your mom. Enjoy the time away with your hottie boyfriend."

Finally, she gave in. "Okay. Thank you. See you in a few days."

"Have fun. And stop worrying about the shop!" Jules called after her as she slid through the doorway, luggage in tow.

Liam rushed around the hood of the Jeep and grabbed the bag from her.

"I can handle it," she protested, even though she actually loved that he'd started doing all the little things like carrying her bag.

"I know you can, but there's no reason you have to," he said.

With a smile she let him take the bag and moved to the passenger side door, which he opened for her to climb up.

"Ready?" he asked once he was behind the wheel and she'd buckled herself in.

"For my boyfriend to meet my mother and my aunt and my cousins for the first time? Probably not."

He smiled. "Don't worry. Mothers love me."

"It'll help that we're going to the distillery first. I can stock up on booze for our overnight stay."

"Is that the reason for the return visit to the distillery?"

"Not really. Just a side benefit. I want to update

Charles. Tell him we solved Gabe's case. He was helpful. And seriously, how much excitement does he get there in the tunnels? I figured he'd appreciate a visit."

"My girlfriend, the ghost whisperer."

She smiled then asked seriously, "You don't mind we're taking a detour to Pine Plains, do you? I know it adds almost an hour to our trip."

"Don't mind at all. Especially since you'll be buying the booze." He grinned.

Two hours later, in the tunnels beneath the distillery, Natalie had to wonder if Liam regretted his answer to her question.

After telling Charles about their success in cracking Gabe's case, and thanking him for his help, she asked, "Is there anything I can do for you before we go?"

The old man's eyes lit and a sly smirk appeared on his wrinkled mouth. "Well, now that you mention it. It's been a long time since I've had my hands on a dame."

Her eyes widened and she wondered if she'd made a major mistake here.

"Wouldn't mind a little dance," he continued. "If G-man over there wouldn't mind too much."

"Um, yeah. I'm sorry. I don't think he'd like that."

"Wait, are you talking about me? What wouldn't I like?" Liam asked.

She waved away his question with one hand while saying, against her better judgment, "Is there anything else?"

He bobbed his head to one side. "There's one thing that's been bothering me that maybe you can take care of."

"What's that?" she asked, hoping she didn't regret it.

"My stash of hooch. I hate the idea of six cases of my finest going to waste. I made it for Jack Diamond. Everyone is all about Dutch but Legs—that's what we called Jack—was the big gun when it came to moving product in these parts. Anyway, he paid for it. I stashed it there for him, and wouldn't you know it, he was killed before he could pick it up. When the shit hit the fan with the feds I decided it was best to leave it there. This is no bathtub gin, mind you. My stuff was some of the best in the country."

"Yours? I have no doubt it'll be good." She smiled, her pulse pounding too fast for her to attempt to do the math on the value of six cases of high-quality Prohibition era moonshine with a connection to a famous mobster.

"It's stashed in an old root cellar that used to be part of this property but when they put the new highway through it became state land. I can show you where it is if you want to come with me."

"I'd love to go with you."

"I visited it over the past couple of years. Not that I can drink it now, but I like to check on it. It brings back memories. But I figure maybe you'd like it. Drink it. Sell it. Give it away. I don't care, just make sure you tell anyone who asks it's Charles Adams's hooch. Once upon a time considered the best in the country. You in? You want it?"

"Yes, I want it. Thank you."

"No sweat, doll. Does this cake eater have a truck that'll fit it all?"

"Don't worry. We'll make it fit."

She moved to follow Charles as Liam stopped her forward progress with a hand on her shoulder. "I'm really going to need you to tell me what you're talking about."

"You'll see soon enough."

"That's what I'm afraid of."

"Hey," Liam said as he stepped up behind her where she stood by the cash register.

After pressing a kiss to her cheek he rested his hands on her hips and leaned his chin on her shoulder.

"What are you up to?"

"Tax day cometh so for better or worse I'm adding my income tax appointment to my calendar." She spun to face him. "I'm worried."

"About?" he asked, holding her tighter against him and making her glad it was five minutes to six when she could officially declare the shop closed for the day.

"Oh, I don't know. Perhaps the secret private sale of dozens of bottles of prohibition moonshine to Gabe's collector friends that earned us over a million dollars." She whispered it even though they were alone.

"There's nothing to worry about."

"How can you say that? Al Capone went down for tax evasion, you know."

"I'm aware, but we're not evading anything. We're going to claim it all. Me as an anonymous donation to the lab and you, slowly, as part of your cash sales. Although I still think you could knock it out all at once if you said it was from selling a rare and valuable book you picked up at a garage sale."

"No."

"Okay, fine. Have it your way. The point is you're paying your fair share of income taxes. We're just doing it while money laundering."

She widened her eyes to prove the point. "Which is also very illegal."

"Is it really though? I mean yes, if we'd made the money selling drugs, very illegal. But we didn't."

"No. Instead we made it selling illegally produced booze."

He held up one finger. "But it was only illegal during Prohibition, which is over so not illegal now."

She was pretty sure that wasn't correct and she'd bet the Bureau of Alcohol, Tobacco and Firearms would agree. But she didn't argue.

Instead she sighed and said, "Fine. We'll call it a gray area."

"There's my girl." He grinned and damned if the combination of his dimple and his calling her *his girl* didn't make her want to drag him back to her bedroom and rip off his clothes.

There was no fighting the attraction between them, even after all these months, so she decided to give in and enjoy it. She took a step forward and was about to close in for a kiss when the front door flew open and a breathless and dirty Jules stopped on the threshold.

"Natalie—"

"What's wrong?"

Silhouetted against the glare of the afternoon early spring sun streaming in the shop door, Jules held up a long dirt covered bone. "Taco just dug this up behind the shop. I think it's—"

"Human," Liam said, moving toward the doorway. "A femur, to be exact."

Natalie's eyes widened. Just when she could stop worrying about money—except for the tax stuff—and she had a hot boyfriend to have lots of celebratory sex with, there couldn't be another murder to solve.

Harper walked in behind Jules and lowered her sunglasses as her gaze hit on the bone still in the girl's hand. "Oh, no. Not again."

"Again?" Natalie squeaked. "What do you mean *again*?"

Behind Harper, Gabe entered and zeroed in on the bone before looking at her. "Sorry. Can't help you. I don't know him—or her."

"I'll explain after I call the sheriff," Harper said.

With the bone held between two dirt covered fingers and with a disgusted look on her face, Jules said, "I'm going to put this thing down and wash up. This is too gross."

As Harper whipped out her cell phone and Jules headed for the bathroom, Natalie turned to look at Liam.

He lifted one shoulder. "At least you've got something else to worry about now. Instead of that other thing."

"Great. Thanks."

"Are you sorry you moved here?" he asked, his hands on her waist again.

She didn't even have to think about that answer. In spite of the ghosts and bones and the near-death experience and the months of financial worries, she could honestly say, "Not even a little bit."

The Séance

It's Natalie and Liam's first Halloween in Mudville with their new friends—of both the human and spiritual variety—but it's not all smooth sailing for the happy couple.

The local ghost community is disgruntled. And it's anyone's guess what could happen when Ghost Gabe convinces Natalie to host an All Hallows' Eve séance at Once Upon a Vine Books and Wine.

Chapter One

IT WAS STARTING TO GET DARK ALREADY AT—Natalie glanced at the time—barely six-thirty. And this was just the beginning. Before she knew it, it would be dusk at four-thirty.

She'd always hated how fall marched so quickly toward the long, cold, dark winter. Although now that she had a boyfriend, maybe it wouldn't be so bad.

Early sunset meant she and Liam would have a good excuse to head to bed and snuggle.

Speaking of sunset...

Just as the sky turned to shades of pink and purple, Gabe walked through—as in *through*—the front door of the shop. But his appearance had nothing to do with the impending darkness. Unfortunately for her, and contrary to popular belief, ghosts didn't only come out at night.

This particular spirit seemed to be active twenty-four seven, proving her supposition that ghosts didn't need to sleep, which is probably why they were always bored and looking for mischief.

"Do you know what day it is?" Gabe asked after making a beeline toward her at the check-out counter.

"Um, Saturday? No. Sunday. Why?"

He rolled his eyes. "I meant the date. Not the day."

"Forgive me but you said *day*, not date."

Days of the week could get fuzzy for her since Once Upon a Vine was open seven days a week—something she was considering reevaluating—but today she actually did know the date. "It's October first. I know because I had to flip the page on my wall calendar."

"And?" he said pointedly.

"And what?" she asked, tired of this game.

She'd finished counting the cash drawer and unpacking that day's deliveries. She'd fed Mr. Darcy—the ungrateful shop cat—and scooped the litter box even though he was outside as much as he was in.

Now she wanted to head to bed—and wait for her hottie boyfriend to join her there after he was done at the lab.

What she did not want to do was play guessing games with a ghost.

"Why isn't the store decorated yet?" Gabe asked.

"Are you my merchandising coordinator now? It's too soon for Christmas decorations. Shoppers get annoyed being bombarded with the holidays this early. I know I do. I'll do all that November first."

In fact, she was really looking forward to her first Christmas here in Mudville at the old train depot. And having a serious boyfriend for the holidays didn't hurt.

She could get a really big tree—which she couldn't do in her former tiny apartment—and Liam could help her set it up in the meeting room. It was going to be so much fun.

"Not Christmas. Halloween," he corrected.

"Oh. Okay. I can do that. I'll go to the farm market and grab a pumpkin and a couple of mums. Maybe some of that ornamental corn to hang on the door. Oh, and some of those corn stalks for either side of the front door. I always liked those. Couldn't get them in the city."

"That's a start, I guess." Gabe scowled.

Was he a decorator now too?

"A start? What else do you want? And why do you even care?"

"Because Halloween is the *big one*. It's like Christmas for ghosts."

"Hmm. I didn't know that."

"Neither did I but everyone else is so excited that it's kind of infectious," Gabe, who was still new at this ghost thing, admitted.

"I guess that makes sense. Actually, this might be a good marketing opportunity. Maybe we should plan some sort of event—"

The tinkling of the bell cut off whatever more Natalie might have said to him.

She was alone in the store so she couldn't be caught talking to herself. Unless it was by Liam, the only other living human to know about her *gift*. And she used that term lightly.

"Hello," Harper sing songed. "I know you're closed but I saw the light on and thought I'd come in and say hi. And maybe grab a bottle of wine?"

Natalie laughed. "Of course. I'm never closed for friends."

"Be careful with that. I might take advantage," Harper grabbed a bottle from the shelf and carried it to the counter.

As Natalie rang up the purchase she said, "I'm glad you stopped in. I was thinking we should maybe do something in the shop for Halloween."

"Yes! Halloween is huge around here. Especially on Main Street. We bought three-hundred and fifty pieces of candy last year to give out at Agnes's house and we ran out just before curfew at seven."

"All right. I guess that settles it. We're doing something... But what?"

"Well, how about trick-or-treating for the kids from four to seven, because where there's kids, there's moms and it won't hurt to draw them to the store. And then after we all shut off our porch lights for the night, do something here for the adults at like eight o'clock?" Harper suggested.

"All right. I'll look for something cool to give out to the kids. Not candy though. Like maybe ghost shaped erasers." She took out her phone and searched. "Oh, look. They have rubber duckies dressed like ghosts. Ooo, glow-in-the-dark ghost buttons. Oh, and pencils with ghost designs."

Harper laughed. "You're really into ghosts."

Natalie realized she was in danger of outing herself and put down her cell. "Oh, you know. Ghosts and Halloween go hand in hand."

Nearby, Gabe snorted. "Good save."

Ignoring him, she asked, "What about for the adult event?"

"I don't know." Harper tapped her finger to her lips

as she thought. "A costume party? Although that could be a lot of work and expense. Maybe a wine tasting, but that's not really Halloweenish."

"Not that anyone asked me but I have an idea," Gabe said.

Unable to answer him, Natalie cut her gaze to Gabe, raising her eyebrows in a *go on* gesture she hoped Harper wouldn't notice.

"A séance," he said.

Now her brows really did fly up.

Séances were right up there with Ouija boards in her list of things she didn't mess with. Not before she'd gained the power to speak to the dead and certainly not now after.

Messing with the occult seemed like asking for trouble.

"Let me google ideas for adult Halloween events," Harper said, unaware of the conversation Natalie was silently having with Gabe.

As Harper whipped out her cell, Gabe continued, "Just hear me out. You can actually talk to the ghosts so your customers will be entertained. And, I didn't want to bring this up, but there's been some grumblings in the ghost community about you. You solved my murder and made sure the police found my next of kin to inherit my stuff, yet you don't even let any of them come in your shop. You owe them something at least. I think letting them have their say just for one night through you at a séance would go a long way in fostering good relations."

The ghost community was upset with her?

That was the most disturbing thing she'd ever heard.

Okay, maybe not the most. Hearing Liam was chopping up cadavers in his lab had been pretty disturbing. But this ranked up there in the top two for sure.

She hated the idea of a séance. But acts of ghostly revenge, and her knowledge of the sheer number of Mudville ghosts who could join those already unhappy with her, scared her more than the idea of hosting a séance.

Drawing in a breath, she turned to Harper. "What do you think about us having a séance here?"

"Oh my God. It's perfect! And historically pertinent for the era of this building. Victorians were obsessed with trying to contact the dead. We might want to cut off attendance at a certain number. This is going to be insanely popular."

"Great. Glad you like the idea," Natalie said with forced enthusiasm while Gabe grinned wide.

For better or worse, it looked like they were doing this.

Chapter Two

"I REALLY WISH YOU WOULD HAVE CANCELED this thing," Liam said to Natalie as she watched the shop's college freshman part-time employee, Jules, sage the meeting room—something she'd learned to do from the local Wiccans.

Natalie, standing next to the small altar she'd set up with amethyst crystals, old Mudville photos and lavender, turned to face her boyfriend. "And I really love that you have expressed your concern daily for the past thirty-one days, but it's going to be fine."

With the séance scheduled to begin in just about ten minutes, Natalie grabbed the lighter she'd bought at the hardware store. As Liam continued to look unhappy, she started lighting the taper candles she'd gotten for tonight.

Thanks to Harper's wine habit Natalie had been able to stick all of the dozen candles in empty wine bottles she'd rescued from Harper's recycling bin.

Scattered around the meeting room the wine bottle candlesticks would illuminate the area nicely once she turned off the overhead lights. They'd add to the spooky atmosphere plus they fit with the theme of a séance held in a wine store.

She flipped the lights off and smiled.

It was perfect. Even the black cat asleep on the sofa added to the ambiance.

Natalie turned to Liam where he leaned back against the long borrowed table that was ringed by eighteen mostly borrowed chairs.

His pout was illuminated by the shop lights coming through the open door.

She pressed a kiss to his lips. "I'm sure it'll be fine. What could go wrong?"

He shook his head. "So many things."

"If anything happens, I'll shut it down. Pretend there aren't any ghosts who want to talk, open that case of cheap Vampire wine I bought and everyone will be happy."

"What if you can't shut it down? Do you personally know all these *ghosts*?" he hissed the last word so Jules and Harper, both now in the shop waiting to open the door at exactly eight p.m., wouldn't hear.

"I don't, but Gabe does. He'll keep them in line."

"So Gabe is going to be your bouncer." One dark brow cocked up.

"You're very cute when you're jealous."

"I'm not jealous."

"Yes, dear. Whatever you say."

As Liam scowled, Gabe swooped through the wall. "Hey. The natives are getting restless out there."

She turned to face Gabe. "The ghosts?"

"Shit. Is he in here?" Liam asked softly.

She nodded.

"I'm *not* jealous," he hissed against her ear before kissing her cheek. "I'll be in the shop," he said before heading through the doorway.

Watching him go, Gabe said, "He's so jealous. It's kind of cute. And the ghosts are fine waiting. They have forever. It's you livings that get impatient."

"I guess we're as ready as we're going to get." She moved to the doorway and said to Jules and Harper, "We can open the door and let everyone sit."

"Yay," Jules squealed as Harper beamed, making a beeline to the door.

Eighteen people took a while to get settled but eventually, everyone was seated around the table, holding hands, which Natalie had read was an acceptable alternative to using a Ouija board, which scared the bejesus out of her.

She had enough to deal with without accidentally summoning something evil. And she definitely didn't need the board to talk to the crowd of ghosts being held outside the building by Gabe.

Communing with the spirits tonight would be the easy part. It was the rest that had required effort. Mainly the research she'd had to do about the whole séance procedure.

She didn't need the showmanship, but the townspeople of Mudville and even her best friends who didn't know about her power, did. They'd expect all the things that went with a typical séance, which she needed to get started now.

According to WikiHow, it was time for the opening invocation to express the intention of this séance.

Seated at the head of the table, Natalie cleared her throat. "Welcome, everyone, and thank you for coming. The purpose of tonight is to allow the spirits who live among us to have their say. Are there any spirits here now who wish to communicate?"

With a nod, Gabe ushered the first ghosts through the wall.

She almost groaned when she saw who had come

forward first. Natalie restrained her reaction and said, "I see, I mean I *feel* the presence of our first two visitors—"

"Can I talk now?" Bob asked.

"For fuck's sake, Bob. You couldn't let me go first?" Bob's wife ranted.

Trying to keep her expression passive, not easy as the couple bickered, Natalie said, "Our visitor's name is Bob. Bob, what do you wish to communicate tonight?"

"Oh, I got plenty to communicate. I've been waiting to tell everyone what I've had to endure for the past twenty years being stuck here with her."

Editing his message in her head, she repeated, "Bob says he passed twenty years ago. Bob, can you tell me the name of the woman who is with you?"

"I'm his wife, Amanda. Not that he ever introduces me. And it's been no picnic for me being dead with him either. Let me tell you."

"Bob is here with his wife Amanda—"

A gasp from one of the men at the table cut her off. "Oh my God. Mom and Dad? You're here?"

Oh, shit. She hadn't anticipated having actual relatives in the audience.

Liam shot Natalie an, *I told you so* glance.

Ignoring Liam she turned her attention to Bob and Amanda's son. "They are here and I can assure you that your parents are spending their afterlife together."

"Aw, that's nice," Harper murmured, since Natalie hadn't painted a complete picture of how their eternity together was going.

"Can I speak with them? I'm Robert Junior."

"I can see if they want to speak to you through me," Natalie offered.

Bob scowled. "We're stuck here together thanks to him. You can tell our son thanks a lot. He had us both buried in the same damn grave. Just to save a buck instead of springing for two plots. Now I have no hope of ever getting away from her."

"Fuck you, Bob," Amanda said, arms crossed as she glared at her husband.

"Fuck you, Amanda. I'm tired of your shit!" he returned.

"It seems we've lost Bob and Amanda. I'm sorry, Robert. But let's move on and see who else wants to talk to us tonight..."

With an amused grin, Gabe went through the wall and returned with his friend from the cemetery. The guy with the two gunshot wounds to the chest.

He dove right in immediately, without introduction, saying, "I want everyone to know I didn't cheat during that card game. Johnson had no reason to shoot me."

"And who are you? What's your name?" Natalie asked.

"Ricky."

Natalie drew in a breath. "Okay. Ricky is here with us tonight and would like you all to know he did not cheat during that card game when he got shot."

There was a gasp from some of the older residents in the room and one grumble from a man who said, "Liar in life. Liar in death."

"Fuck you, Buck." Ricky scowled before whipping his gaze to Natalie. "You tell him that for me."

"Um, Ricky disagrees with that opinion."

There was a snort from Buck after which Ricky said, "Fuck this. I'm outta of here."

Natalie's eyes widened as she watched him storm out through the wall.

She probably should have predicted this night could devolve into a spiritual bitch fest. If the trend of the first few continued, that's what it was going to be. And there was still a line of ghosts waiting to get inside to air their grievances. The next of which Gabe was escorting inside.

"All right, next..."

Half a dozen ghost later and Natalie missed the earlier fireworks of Bob, Amanda and Ricky.

She'd had two recently dead spirits who only wanted to say hello to their relatives, who weren't in attendance. Then there were four much, *much* older spirits who'd banded together in solidarity and come to lodge a complaint that their gravesites weren't being properly maintained in the old graveyard on the outskirts of town.

One glance around the room told Natalie that she was losing the attention of the crowd. A few remained rapt, waiting for the next revelation. But most looked just plain bored and she didn't blame them.

She had to do something.

"Spirits, can you make your presence known to us in a physical way?" She glanced at Gabe, then tipped her head toward the gathered crowd of livings. "Give us a demonstration that you are here. Let us feel your *ghostly hand* upon us."

Rolling his eyes, Gabe mumbled, "All right. I hear you. Real subtle, by the way."

He walked to the edge of the circle, extended his hand and swept it through the nearest person. The woman gasped and shivered.

"Something touched me." She glanced around at those nearest her. "It touched me!"

Natalie lifted her chin to Gabe, who sighed and walked around the circle. In a ghostly approximation of the kid's game Duck, Duck, Goose, he swept his hand through the head of each and every person seated there, including Liam.

Like a wave, the gasps and shocked murmurs moved through the group and just like that, no one looked bored anymore. Liam looked annoyed, but he'd deal.

With a twitch of a smile that she quelled since this was a solemn, serious occasion, she said, "Are there more spirits here? Please step forward..."

Chapter Three

After the ghosts had had their say and dispersed, and the guests were ushered out and the door locked, Jules turned to Natalie. "That was absolutely amazing! How did you do all that?"

She'd prepared for this. With a shrug, she said, "It was easy. It just took lots of research into the people buried here in the local cemeteries. And also the archived obituaries from the paper so I knew who died, how and when."

"You had me fooled," Harper said with a shake of her head. "You ever need a side gig, you could take that show on the road and earn a living."

Natalie laughed. "Thanks but no thanks." She'd had her hands full already just with the ghosts of Mudville.

"Well, great job. I think everyone had a great time."

"And we sold out of sage bundles and they put quite a dent in the crystals and Tarot cards," Jules added.

"That's all thanks to you, Jules, for having the idea to keep the shop open after the séance was over."

"Grab 'em while you got 'em. I knew people would want to buy things right after." Jules grinned.

Harper held up the bottle she'd just bought. "You were right and now it's time for me to take my purchase and head home. Want a ride?" Harper asked Jules.

"Sure. Thanks."

After they'd said goodnight and the door had been once again locked behind them, Liam emerged from the meeting room with a cardboard wine box filled with the burned down candles and wax-spattered wine bottles.

He set the box on the floor behind the register and reached for Natalie, then stopped. "We alone?"

"Yes, we're alone."

"I figured Gabe would hang around for a postmortem about the event."

"He'll probably want to do that in the morning. Tonight, he's at a ghost party in the cemetery."

"There's a party?"

She nodded. "Apparently Halloween is a really big deal for ghosts."

"So you're saying we have the place all to ourselves?" Liam pressed closer, wrapping his arms around her.

"Yes. Why? What did you have in mind?" she asked, even though she already knew, thanks to the hard length she felt between them.

"I'm thinking we can have a private party. Just the two of us." He dipped his head and ran his lips down her throat.

"What got you all worked up?" she asked.

Liam was passionate, and their sex life was great, but he didn't usually get physical in the middle of the shop with the lights still on.

"Seeing you do your ghost thing tonight in front of everybody. It was kind of hot." He dipped the tip of his tongue into her ear.

"Oh, really?" she said as a shiver ran through her.

"Mmm-hmm." His teeth scraped against her throat and her eyes drifted closed.

"Maybe I should do the ghost thing in public more often."

He pulled back and gave her a look. "I think once a year will be enough."

"Okay. Only once a year for that." She tipped her head toward the meeting room. "But definitely *not* only once a year for this." She let her gaze sweep down his body.

"Definitely not." He grabbed her hand and tugged her toward her apartment in the back of the building as she hit the switch to kill the shop lights on her way past.

Gabe could have his all-night rave in the cemetery. She was perfectly content to head to bed for their own little party for two.

In fact, it would be more than fine with her if this—all of this—became their annual Halloween tradition.

Graveyard Secrets Series

BY CAT JOHNSON

Cadaver Lab: A Romantic Comedy...with corpses

Cadaver Lab 2: Ghostly Hearts & Body Parts

Cadaver Lab 3: Spirited Shenanigans

Cadaver Lab 4: Grave's Anatomy

WELCOME TO
Mudville
NEW YORK
Bethany's House
Cadaver Lab
Honey Buns
Library
Agnes's House
STATION
Once Upon a Time Books & Wine
Variety Store
Main Street
DINER
BURGERS MALTS
Red's Shop
RIP
Mudville House
Mudville Diner
Rose's
Muddy River
Muddy River Inn
Morgan Farm Market
"Mudville" by Cat Johnson inspired by Unadilla, NY

Behind the Book

Readers often ask writers where we get ideas. The answer is *everywhere*. Seriously, I never know what is going to spur a concept for a new book or series. Case in point—*Cadaver Lab*. Where did *that* come from? Let me tell you.

I spend at least an hour a day chatting with other professionals about business stuff related to publishing, writing and marketing. During one of these chats there was a guy, Justin, who knew a ton about social media marketing but didn't seem to be an author. Finally, someone asked what he did for a living and his answer was social media for—wait for it—a cadaver lab.

A cadaver lab?! Oh. My. God. My heart sped. My mind whirled. It was like angels sang and my writing muse awakened.

Immediately I knew I wanted to write this book. And it was going to be fun and funny, and probably more than a little bit irreverent because writing a romantic comedy set amongst corpses would have to be, right?

I pawed into Justin's bio, found the link for his company and did a deep dive into all the videos posted. They were educational and, once I got past the dead body part, really interesting.

Even better—be still my romance writing heart—there was a hot doctor leading us through the presentations, primed and ready to be the inspiration for my next book boyfriend hero.

The cadaver lab idea hit right at a time that ghosts seemed to be having a moment, at least on the small screen. The CBS show "Ghosts" is my new favorite comedy series. I'm pretty sure its success is what spurned "Not Dead Yet" on ABC and "School Spirits" streaming on Paramount+.

Was it fate or coincidence that delivered this idea to me at what feels like the exact right time? Who knows? But it seemed like a perfect moment to write this story.

And where else would I set this unconventional, off-beat story than in my favorite quirky small town, Mudville.

As usual when I'm writing about Mudville, which is

not so secretly based on the real town where I currently live, I use actual locations.

The train depot that becomes Natalie's shop exists. It's a couple of blocks from my house and currently empty and in need of some tender loving care.

The adorable old train depot is next to a vacant building that had operated as a warehouse for the railroad that still runs today, though for freight trains only.

That warehouse is the inspiration for Liam's lab location.

For history buffs, the rumor of Dutch's treasure is real, as is the distillery and the New York Times article about it. Charles Adams did work there for Patrick Ryan and later buy the property, but his stash of hooch and his ghost are my invention.

Finally, that margarita song? Totally real!

That's it. The *Cadaver Lab* origin story and proof inspiration really can come in any and all forms. I hope you had as much fun reading as I had writing.

 *Cat*

About the Author

A top 10 *New York Times* and nine-time *USA Today* bestselling contemporary romance author, Cat Johnson writes hot alpha heroes (who often wear cowboy or combat boots) and the sassy heroines brave enough to love them.

Known for her creative marketing, Cat has sponsored bull riding cowboys and promoted romance using bologna.

She writes full time from a Queen Anne Victorian in a small town in upstate New York suspiciously like Mudville where she tends to her backyard chickens and too many cats.

Find more information visit catjohnson.net.

Join the email list at catjohnson.net/news.